CROSSING LINES

MELANIE WEISS

ROSEHIP PUBLISHING

Cover Art by Jana Malecek
Author photo by Alyssia Evans
Cover Design by Pixel Studios
Edited by Kathryn F. Galán, Wynnpix Productions

Published by Rosehip Publishing, Oak Park, Illinois
www.melanie-weiss.com

This is a work of fiction. Names, characters, places, brands, media, and incidents are either the product of the author's imagination or are used fictitiously. Any resemblance to similarly named places or to persons living or deceased is unintentional. Crossing Lines is suggested for ages 14 and up, due to mild sexual situations.

PRINT ISBN 978-0-9886-0985-3

This book is dedicated to the seventeen teachers and students of Marjory Stoneman Douglas High School in Parkland, Florida, who lost their lives and to the seventeen others who were injured on February 14, 2018, at the hands of a former student armed with an AR-15-style semi-automatic rifle.
We honor these beautiful souls who were killed on that day whenever we choose kindness and act toward others with compassion.

The Second Amendment of the United States Constitution reads: "A well-regulated Militia, being necessary to the security of a free State, the right of the people to keep and bear Arms, shall not be infringed."

–Passed by Congress on September 25, 1789
Ratified on December 15, 1791
The first ten amendments form the Bill of Rights

Sung to the tune of "Twinkle, Twinkle, Little Star":

Lockdown, lockdown, lock the door
Shut the lights off, say no more
Go behind the desk and hide
Wait until it's safe inside
Lockdown, lockdown, it's all done
Now it's time to have some fun!

—Taped to the chalkboard in a Somerville, Massachusetts
kindergarten class, June 2018

GLOSSARY OF TERMS

BFN: Bye for now

IM Kick/Drill: A mix of kicking, swimming, and drilling of four strokes (breaststroke, butterfly [fly], backstroke and front crawl.)

IMO: In my opinion

IU2U: It's up to you

MAGA: "Make America Great Again" is a campaign slogan used in American politics by Donald J. Trump during his presidential campaigns and throughout his presidency, often displayed on red baseball caps.

Medley: Combination of four different swimming styles into one race.

P-I-T-A: Pain in the ass

PR: Personal Record

Promposal: This usually involves a special action that took some thought and time to prepare, rather than simply asking a person, "Do you wanna go to prom with me?"

JANUARY 6, 2018

BRANDON

"Well, that sucked!" I tell Coach after I botch what, on most any other day of the year, would be my best race. He pats me on my back, and together we study the clock above the deep-end bleachers.

"Is there molasses in the pool today?" Coach Cam quips.

"I wish that could be my excuse." I keep my eyes glued to the race results, since I'm afraid to look at the disappointment on his face.

He walks away, and I know to stay out of his sight for the rest of the swim meet between our Chicago-area club team, the Dolphins, and our toughest league rival, the Aquaducks.

I grab a small towel from my bag, briefly swipe at my soggy Speedo, and then sit my wet butt on the cold metal bench. I scrunch my hair with the towel, shaking my head as I recall how I stubbed my toe on a turn and let that sensation slow me down. *Stupid, stupid, stupid.*

"Hey, keep your drips to yourself," I hear from behind me and turn around. Alli is wiping her right cheek with her hand to erase the droplets I let loose.

"Sorry, but you know. Fourth place might as well be last, right?"

"You usually have the 200 free locked up," she says with a smirk. "You're slipping."

"Ha, ha, Miss 'I just smoked the 100 fly.' I missed third by a quarter of a second."

"Ouch!" She eases herself next to my bag on the bench. I brush it to the floor and slide closer to her.

"Hey, are you going to Simone's birthday party tonight?"

"Yes, Brandon," she scolds. "Of course, I'm going to my best friend's eighteenth birthday party."

I stare at Alli. Slips of wet hair cling to the side of her face. Even though we're five months away from high school graduation, I've had a raging crush on her since she sat down next to me in Ms. Albert's second-period freshman algebra class at Edgewood High School.

Looking at her is like staring into a Florida sunset in July. Blazing glorious, and hot as hell. Her brown hair is stick-straight, and her eyes are brown with a hint of green. She has more impressive biceps than mine. And she owns the 100-yard fly.

"Are you going with Ricardo?" I ask as we watch the meet wrap up and grab our swim bags to head toward the showers.

"Nope," she says flatly. "We broke up over winter break."

I turn quickly toward her as she hoists her swim bag over her shoulder. "I'm driving to Simone's party, so if you need a ride, I could swing by and get you."

"You sure?"

I nod a little too eagerly. "I'll pick you up at eight."

"That would be great. I'll text you my address," she adds before disappearing into the women's locker room.

I know I should be pissed that I didn't even place today, but I have more important things on my mind now. I hope Alli hasn't put me in the friend zone. At 8 p.m. sharp, I'm going to walk up to her front door, ring the doorbell, and make nice with the parents rather than text a "*HERE*" from my car.

In my book, we're about to go on our first date.

* * *

ALLI

I sit on the hard, wooden bench in the locker room and wring water from my ponytail. The door opens and closes three times before Simone steps in.

"Simone!" I wave and point to the spot beside me.

"I need a hot shower. It was freezing on the deck." Simone shows me the goosebumps on her right arm then pulls her towel tighter around her and skootches next to me. She slowly rolls off her swim cap and grabs a T-shirt from her bag, which she wraps around her tight French braids, then ties the sleeves around the back of her neck. She looks ridiculous, but I don't blink. I've witnessed her cotton T-shirt hair-drying trick a thousand times.

"Great race," she says, her legs splayed next to mine. Although Simone and I are both about 5'8", her legs are longer and more muscular than mine. According to Cam, they're her secret weapon. When he shouts "You're up, Legs" during relay practice, there's no mistaking who he's talking to.

"You too. Great relay," I respond, anxious to loop her in on what happened five minutes ago.

She tightens the knot behind her neck. "What's up?"

"So, Brandon is picking me up, and we're driving to your party tonight. He just asked me."

"Girl, that Brandon is so goddamn obvious. You know he's had a thing for you since that math class you took together. He always gets that goofy grin when you two are talking." She flashes a sly smile.

I nod. Back when we would go over equations together in study hall, I could practically feel the heat coming off him. I was flattered by his flirting, even though it threw me off balance. I knew I couldn't be distracted from swimming if I was going to land a college scholarship, so I told him I wasn't allowed to date, just to keep him from thinking we could happen. He was like a tiger hunting his prey. I kept my distance. It was just all too dangerous.

"After he dated Darcy in the middle of her long list of college guys she was banging, I just never thought I would want to date him. But maybe I'm ready for this now. I mean, what's not to like?" I smile as I think about his ocean-blue eyes and how his bronze-tinged hair hangs a bit long around his angular face, the perfect frame for his chiseled features.

"You two were destined to be a thing. So now it's happening. Finally!" Simone briskly stands to head for the showers and hugs the towel tightly around her, keeping the T-shirt on her head. The goosebumps have disappeared, and her dark skin is now glistening and smooth. "And that body will not disappoint!" she hollers as she turns the corner.

I guess it is time I let myself go out with a bad boy. And trust me, Brandon Paulson is maybe one notch into the bad-boy meter, so I am starting off slow here. Ricardo Ralen, the only high school boy I ever dated, plays first-chair violin in the orchestra and listens to classical music. He's smart and sweet and never complained about me being crazy busy and always tired. He didn't mind just chilling on the sofa weekend nights, watching movies and eating buttery microwave popcorn from the same huge bowl. It took us a year to get to third base, which is as far as it went. When I sent him a rambling "it's not you, it's me" breakup text last month, I don't think he even cared that much.

I've checked all the boxes required of me and accepted a scholarship to a Division I university, where I'm going to work my ass off, juggling competitive swimming and being a college student while figuring out what I want to do with my life (things I like: biology, English lit, and psychology).

I've heard the drinking scene is practically nonexistent for us college athletes, so I'm giving up a lot of fun. It sucks to think about the parties I'll have to miss so I can get out of bed for swim practice before the sun is even up. Now, for these few months before I go to preseason training, it's going to be all about Alli. And Alli wants Brandon.

* * *

BRANDON

I'm wearing my favorite light blue T-shirt, the one that Darcy once said matches my eyes. But since it's January, I have to throw on my heaviest winter parka, the olive-green one that has no style but keeps me from freezing my ass off.

"Mom, I'm taking your car now," I announce loudly as I snatch the keys off the hook by the back door.

"Wait, Brandon. Did you walk Astor?" Mom yells from the living room.

"Mom, no. I've gotta go. I'm going to be late."

"Brandon. Walk her around the block. It won't take long. You know, on weekends, I am not on dog duty."

"That's funny, Mom." But I know she has no idea what I'm talking about.

I run around the block with Astor, stopping for a brief few seconds so she can pee on a tree.

Jumping in the car, I glance at the dashboard clock and realize I'm going to be ten minutes late to get Alli. I wanted everything to go perfect tonight. I send a quick text before I back the car out of the driveway.

OMW

I roll through a few stop signs and drive with a heavy foot on the gas. I park in her driveway at 8:07 p.m. and jump out of my car to meet the parents.

As Alli opens the front door, I admire how she's busting out of her fuchsia top.

"What's wrong? Is it the shirt?" she asks, catching me glancing at the tight, bright V-neck.

"What? No? You look fantastic," I say a little too enthusiastically.

"You're laughing at me." She turns around as if prepared to march upstairs to change.

Oh, God. Doesn't she know how hot she looks? Now she thinks I'm a dick. Way to go.

"I'm not. I swear."

"Simone gave it to me for my birthday," she says, angling back in my direction. "It's her favorite color. I never wear it, but I figured, on her birthday, I'd show her how much I like it. Tomorrow, it's going in the Goodwill pile."

She is so clueless about how completely gorgeous she looks. I'd be happy if she wore that shirt every day.

She eases into her navy jacket, grabs a small gift bag from a table next to the front door that's piled with mail, and then steps beside me on the front stoop.

"You're lucky," she says as she locks the door behind her. "My mom and Ray, he's my stepdad, took my brothers out to dinner."

"Oh. And I was all ready to charm them."

"Well, no need now." We walk down the steps toward my car.

"What did you get Simone?" I ask, eyeing the bag she's carrying.

"A pink Magic 8 ball. It comes with a little pink silk pillow to rest on. I found it on eBay. They're hard to come by. I thought it would be fun for us to mess around with. "Like, *It is certain. It is decidedly so. Outlook good,*" she drones.

"Well, there's also *Don't count on it.*"

"Or *Reply hazy.* What does that mean, really?" Alli says this like it's a serious question she wants to ponder as we stand in front of the passenger car door.

"That's a cool idea. My sisters had one way back. The regular black version. I got Simone a $20 gift card to Amazon but added a link to my favorite goggles. She's always making fun of them, but secretly I know she really wants a pair."

"You mean those space-age mirrored things you wear? I've always thought they were super pricy because of how flashy they are."

"My Socket Rockets? Nah, they're $15. Hey, how old are your brothers?" I open the car door for her, hoping my gentlemanly gesture proves we are on a date.

"They're eight. Technically they're my half-brothers because my mom had them with my stepdad. My dad lives in the city." She drops into the passenger seat. "They definitely take over the house, though, with their nonstop energy," she adds, starting to close the car door.

When we are both settled, I turn to her. "They sound really great. Maybe I can meet them. Kids love me. I've done so much babysitting and math tutoring that I was able to pay almost the whole cost for my school Spanish exchange trip last summer."

"Wow. That's cool. To be honest, it's no fricking fairy tale in my house. I cannot tell you how often I feel like the fifth wheel on the family minivan. Like I'm crashing this family unit." Alli takes a deep breath. "Most of the time, there just isn't a car for me to use or the desire on anyone's part to get me where I need to go, since it often means bundling my twin brothers in the back seat, which is an ordeal in itself. I guess that's a long way of saying I appreciate the ride."

I nod, even though I don't want to be thought of as her chauffeur tonight. I change the subject.

"So is your dad remarried, too?"

She glances over at me and shakes her head but says nothing more, so I leave the heaviness to sit in the air. Awkward.

* * *

ALLI

Well, this conversation has gone downhill fast. Though I admit my rant didn't set up a positive vibe. I sit and stew a few minutes in the buzzkill subject Brandon threw into the mix.

As much as I try, I can't live up to my dad's need for me to be his constant ray of sunshine. He got a raw deal, and the one-bedroom apartment where he lives above his pawnshop is a constant reminder of that.

It all started off golden with him and my mom. He owned a bar-type restaurant in Chicago with a college friend that was pulling in good money when my mom got pregnant with me. My dad ran the front of the house, dealing with employees and food orders and drunk customers, while his friend ran the back of the house, which was the business side of things.

Soon after I was born, the unpaid bills started piling up, so my dad asked his brother the accountant to do an audit. They quickly found out dad's business partner was using one of the restaurant's credit cards to help fund his two hundred-person black-tie wedding and Caribbean honeymoon. A "loan," he called it. So, the restaurant closes, my dad gets depressed, my mom blames him and then leaves him. I was barely two years old.

After a few minutes of uncomfortable quiet fills the car, I peer over at Brandon. "My dad used to own a restaurant, but that business went south. So now he has a pawnshop in Chicago," I say, going full-out honest. "It was his Uncle Joe's, but he got Parkinson's and couldn't run it anymore, so my dad took it over."

"I don't think I've ever been in a pawnshop. But I've seen that show on TV. *Pawn Stars*. Have you seen it?"

"No. Not my thing." I stare out the window.

"Where in Chicago?"

"It's in Logan Square not far from Bucktown. So, have you been to this trampoline place before?" I ask, craning my neck to inspect the unfamiliar neighborhood we've driven into and wanting to change the subject.

"Yeah, once, a few years ago. It's just up past the next light. I am so glad Simone invited me. And I've been wanting us to hang out for a while, but, you know, Ricardo and stuff."

"Stuff like Darcy?"

"She's so in the past, though. What do you think of her?"

"For one thing, she probably spends like $60 a month just on eyelash extensions. That's so not my style. We're completely different."

He laughs loud. "You and Darcy BFFs? No, that I cannot picture."

I start to chuckle. "You do know that she wore a white, ruffled thong bikini bottom when she was babysitting the Nowicki kids last summer at the local pool? My brothers play with Justin Nowicki, so that story made the rounds. My mom even asked me if I knew her."

I look over at Brandon as he starts to blush and decide I'm having too much fun.

"Oh, and that she was doing handstands in the shallow end," I add gleefully.

"Wow, tiger, your claws are out," he says sharply, as he pulls into the huge lot outside Sky Zone.

I realize I took it too far. I know she's a piece of work, but she was his girlfriend. I defer to his admonition.

"Sorry. My bad." I feel a little bit guilty that I was so gossipy. As much as I don't respect her, I am impressed by how Brandon defended her questionable honor.

* * *

BRANDON

It ends up being ten of us who meet up at the trampoline park. We find our own section of mats away from the younger kids and dodgeball players. I can't help but notice there's nothing logical about the color palette in here. Large black trampoline squares are outlined with what looks like yellow police tape. Around the yellow outlines are alternating borders of bold orange or blue bumpers. There's a strobe light flashing white dots right next to the large area we've gravitated toward.

To add to my disorientation, the music is super-loud and completely awful. What heavy metal stoner picks their playlist? Even with hard rock thumping in the background, the best thing about trampoline parks is it's impossible not to laugh the whole time. So, we jump from section to section, cracking up.

I launch all six feet of me into a sad excuse for a backflip I hope nobody sees. The silver cross I wear on a long chain hits me in the face as it escapes from inside my shirt. I twist it so it trails down my back and continue bouncing.

As I topple backward for the hundredth time, Alli hops over to my side, offering a hand to pull me up. I grab it and lightly tug her toward me on the mat.

"*Hey!*" she exclaims. Her eyes widen with surprise.

She lands next to me, our arms and legs knocking together, as we shift awkwardly to try to stand on the unsteady surface despite the bouncing all around us. We give up the plan to get back on our feet and just let go, our bodies swaying left to right in rhythm along with the jumping bodies that flit overhead.

Lying next to her, I yield to the sensations that reverberate below. Alli's hair is splayed out on the mat, and her face is aglow with laughter. Our friend, Daryll, jumps over us both, and after he lands hard inches from her head, Alli curls her body into mine. I fold her in my arms to protect her from his next wild move and the circus that is whirling all around us. As I hold her, I think boldly how I want Alli every way there is to want someone.

Too soon, she pushes away from me, bolts to her feet, and heads over to where Simone and Wendy are doing front flips.

As she floats farther from my orbit, I start to deflate. It's not *wanting*, I admit. I need to be with her.

* * *

ALLI

None of us have our cell phones. They are all sealed in lockers near the front desk. But I start to get nervous that it's getting late. In my house, curfew is 11:30 p.m. I've gotten in trouble for coming home even fifteen minutes late. And trouble in my house means being grounded, aka no social life that next weekend. I've been grounded twice, and it sucks bigtime.

"Hey, Simone." I wave at her. She jumps over my way, and I grab her arm. There's no use talking over AC/DC's "Back in Black," so I tap on her Fitbit watch to check the time. Seeing it's 10:50 p.m., I pantomime to her an "Oh shit, I gotta go," as I shake my hands wildly and then scan the jumping cage for Brandon.

I look and look but don't see him, so I bounce to the edge to get a clearer view. I finally spot him at the far corner, sitting down and talking to Seth. I jump down from the mats and jog over to where they're sitting. Through the mesh, I poke at Brandon's back.

"Hey, can we leave now? I have to get home," I say as I catch my breath.

He turns around, his hair all askew. He nods and, after saying a few words to Seth, descends the few steps to meet me on the rubberized floor.

"Sorry I didn't warn you. I need to be home by 11:30," I explain.

"No worries. I'm pretty beat. All this jumping is a huge workout."

I raise my right hand to pat down his hair where it is sticking up. "That's better," I say, admiring my work. "Is my hair sticking up, too?" I smooth mine lightly on both sides with my fingers.

He stares at me with those damn stars in his eyes again.

"No," he says. "It's perfect."

We grab our jackets and phones from the lockers and head to the parking lot.

"My mom and stepdad can act like complete tyrants when it comes to my curfew," I complain to Brandon, dropping into the passenger seat. I mimic my mom's standard line: "We need our sleep. We can't be up worrying about you and then function during the day with all we have going on."

"She's harsh, huh?" Brandon cranks the heat up in the car.

"I get it. My two brothers are like nonstop tornados, and they suck up all the oxygen in the house. I feel like there are so many times when the things I need become just a problem to be solved. When I turned eighteen, I was supposed to get a later curfew, but then, well..." I realize I'm heading to a story I am not ready to tell. "It hasn't happened yet." I end my confession.

"I guess I'm lucky my sisters paved the way for me to have no curfew," Brandon says. "Maura was always hanging out with her best friend, who lived two blocks away. My mom and dad were friends with her parents, so they kinda knew what she was up to. Kelly was the wild one, usually coming home after 1 a.m., completely stoned. My parents got so tired worrying about her that I get a free pass as long as I don't pull a Kelly."

"And you haven't, huh?"

"No. I need my sleep. Though my parents know she's shared her weed with me a few times. Well, more than a few. But always during the summer off-season, so it doesn't count, right?"

"I hate pot," I say. "I did it once and acted like a complete idiot in front of my friend Cindy and her older brother. I was the opposite of cool."

I surprise myself. Why am I spilling all these secrets with Brandon? Why does just sitting next to him make my mouth spout out everything cycling through my head?

"I find that hard to believe," Brandon says, bringing me back to the moment. He pulls up to the curb in front of my house.

"Trust me." I loop my right fingers on the car door handle. "It was not pretty. It's the last thing I should be doing, anyway, so it's good I hated it."

"That's true. You know what Coach always says."

"Yeah, make good choices," I reply, dropping my voice down two octaves to sound more Cam-ish, while I mimic one of his many mantras. "He wants us to be as boring as possible."

Brandon turns off the ignition, and suddenly an awkward silence envelops the car. My mind starts to reel. *Are we going to kiss now?* I realize I want us to. A lot!

I glance over at him to say, "Thanks for the ride…"

He leans over to me before I can get my words out and kisses my lips sweetly and lightly. My heart sings. We've flirted around the edges of our attraction for so long. Now, there's no denying it. The electric charge between us is intense and beautiful, and we both want to explore it.

"Good night, Alli," he says softy as he slides back behind the steering wheel.

I stumble thunderstruck out of the bucket seat. My heart is thumping loudly. It was just one short kiss, but it ignites a fire in me I can't deny. I lean against the front door inside our foyer and check my phone. I've made it home with four minutes to spare.

I walk into the kitchen for a glass of water. Brandon didn't act showy or cocky for a minute. There was a lot about him I liked before tonight. Now, I have to admit, there's even more that intrigues me.

* * *

BRANDON

I wake up the next morning thinking about Alli. I really want to cement this. *Us.*

I grab my phone from the nightstand.

Wanna study at Starbucks later? I text her.

KK, she texts back. *1?*

I thumbs-up her text and jump out of bed, hoping I have a decent clean shirt to throw on. That's one of the shitty things about having parents who met in the Marines. Not only do I have to make my bed with tight corners before breakfast every day. I also do my own laundry, fold it, and put it away, all on their schedule. Sunday is laundry day.

I get to Starbucks a few minutes early and see Alli has found a table facing the huge front window, her head already buried in her laptop. I walk up and tap her shoulder.

She looks up at me, her eyes sparkling under the fluorescent lights, and throws out a soft, "Hey."

"Coffee?" I ask, as I drop my backpack on the chair. I'm psyched she was able to get us one of the spacious wooden tables, so we can spread out our stuff.

Her hair is pulled into a loose ponytail, and I notice right away she's got mascara and lip gloss on for our study date. I take it as a good sign that both of us did more than roll out of bed and throw on sweats.

"I drink tea," she says. "But I can get it. I just wanted to snag this table before someone else did."

"I think I can afford to buy you hot water and some wet leaves," I joke.

"Okay, then. Green, please." Alli smiles up at me.

I jump into the queue behind a mom and her two young sons. One tugs on her pale blue sweater, while the other points to the glass case and pleads, "Please, Mom." After they both score a white-frosted cake pop decorated with colored sprinkles, it's finally my turn at the counter. I place our order, and a few minutes later, Alli and I are sitting next to each other. I sip my coffee, black, as she ignores her tea and types furiously.

"What are you working on?"

"A psych paper. What about you?"

"AP Calc," I answer, opening my laptop.

She smiles. "Fancy!"

"It's actually a great class. Don't ask me to read a four hundred-page book or find my way out of a paper bag in Spanish, but give me a graphing calculator, and it just feels like I'm where I should be."

Alli looks at me for a quick minute then quietly mumbles, "Wow, so you're a math geek." She returns to her laptop and starts typing away.

Suddenly, her head pops up, and she studies me warily.

I feel unsettled by her wide-eyed gaze.

"What? Do I have food on my face or something?" I wildly swipe at my mouth, cheeks, nose.

"No. It's just you said you suck at Spanish. But didn't you go to Spain last summer? Your Spanish can't be that bad."

"*Siempre arruino los tiempos verbales. ¿A quién se le ocurrió esa cosa masculina-femenina de todos modos?*" I respond in my flat, halting accent.

"Oh, that was painful," she says with a huge grin. "And I agree. The male-female tense thing is confusing. Did you get better at it during your trip, though? I would think it would be so helpful, when you get to speak Spanish in Spain."

"*Un poco.*" I rock my palm back and forth. "Spain was awesome. Barcelona is the most amazing place." I pick up my phone and pull up photos from the La Sagrada Familia. "This is a church they have been working on for, like, 150 years. Check out those gargoyles. It was designed by this guy, Gaudi, whose stuff is all over the city." I scroll through a bunch more photos, our heads bent over the small screen.

After we spend probably too much time sharing photos and then earbuds to watch our favorite YouTube videos (hers: Ariana Grande and some South Korean white fluffball dog named Pongki; mine: comic stand-up bits by John Mulaney), interspersed with a small amount of schoolwork, that laundry thing starts to nag at me.

"Alli, I gotta go. Do you need a ride?"

"Nah, I'm good. Simone is coming by soon, and we're going to go to Ulta."

"What's that?" I ask, clueless.

"Really, dude? It's the makeup place *right next door*." She shakes her head.

I shrug. "Well, have fun while I do my laundry. Parents' orders." I explain how having a mom and dad who are ex-Marines means if I don't get my laundry done, I will be stuck home next weekend sitting on the couch between my parents, watching the History Channel. "The highlight of their evening is when they eat bowls of mint chocolate chip ice cream in front of the TV," I add in all seriousness.

As I stick my laptop in my backpack and hoist the strap over my right shoulder, she says, "I feel your pain. Hey, if your parents are ex-military, how come they let you and your sister smoke pot?"

I stand stiffly and digest the question. "My parents are Libertarians, so, for them, as long as I'm not hurting anyone, I can smoke all the pot I want."

"That's crazy."

I ignore her comment, as I don't want to get into it, but to me it makes perfect sense.

"Peace out," I joke and flip her a V peace sign. I grab my empty coffee cup and toss it in a nearby garbage can.

"You're such a nerd," she says.

"Ouch," I proclaim, playfully clutching my wounded heart as I head toward the door.

The chilly air is made bearable by the sun shining down from a cloudless sky. My phone pings in seconds. I peek down at the message. Alli has sent me a smiley face emoji with black eyeglasses and two buck teeth.

I start to scroll through my emojis to find the perfect response, but then a second message appears. Another bucktooth emoji, but this one has pink eyeglasses and a hairbow.

I study the pair of goofy smiley faces. If this is what it means to be a nerd, then sign me up!

* * *

ALLI

I admire how Brandon's jeans hug his tight butt as he walks away. I watch him push open the glass door, holding it for a woman who nods at him as she rushes in quickly.

I pick up my phone to text him a few emojis and then open up Chrome. I punch the word "libertarian" into the search bar then scroll around for a while, reading and learning about this political philosophy. I'd never heard of it before, but apparently his parents take it very seriously.

Thirty minutes later, Simone walks up as I'm putting the final touches on my psych paper. "Ready?" she asks. She has no makeup on, not a stitch, which is not like her. That means she is ready to have the Benefit pro at Ulta paint her face.

Makeup-free Simone is so pretty, which I'm sure she knows, too. Thin, perfectly manicured eyebrows that arch just so over her dancing, wide-set brown eyes. A slightly broad nose. Her dark skin clear and radiant.

"I think Brandon is a Libertarian," I blurt out. "Is that weird?"

She laughs. "Okay. Like he's pro-liberty. Yeah, that is so weird."

"No, like a fringe-y no-rules type guy. Guns, drugs are okay. Taxes, not so much. That's what he says his parents are."

"Did you ask him if he believes all that shit, too?" She stares at me.

"I didn't want to get all serious. But we have to talk about it. Gun control is something I really care about."

"Alli, you're not dating his parents. It sounds like their thing, not his."

"But you know what happened to my dad last summer. At the pawnshop."

"You mean the robbery? Yeah, of course. That was so scary," Simone whispers as she drops slowly into the chair next to me.

"Not just the robbery. Having the gun cocked at his temple while he emptied the register. It really fucked him up. Now, he pops anti-anxiety meds the minute he wakes up and sleep meds every night."

"Oh, shit! I didn't know that."

"Well, I don't like to talk about it. The guy who robbed him got maybe $300 and some emerald rings, but my dad has never been the same since. I just don't want to disrespect my dad and be dating someone who doesn't get me."

"You should tell me these things. Do you worry he's addicted? Is that part of what's stressing you out?"

I start to answer but instead shake my head, not wanting this thought to take residence inside it. "The meds are helping him deal with the trauma," I explain, which feels liberating to say out loud. "He needs them. He'll quit when he gets past this." This simple truth reassures me as much as Simone.

I start to stand and go but my chest tightens as I think about how fucked up he has been since the robbery. How fragile he can be. How Simone just called him an addict. "He gets his meds from a doctor who would know if there was a problem," I add, needing to convince us both.

Simone nods, either in agreement or solidarity, I can't tell which. "Hey, did they ever catch the guy?" she asks.

I shake my head. "Nope."

"I just hate what that robbery did to your dad, too." We both stand up, and she burrows her body into mine. Around us, people keep drinking lattes and typing away on laptops. I let myself melt into her shoulder and think back to that June day when everything was so routine, so normal, and then, within seconds, it wasn't.

Simone steps away gently and puts her arms on my shoulders. "Alli. You need to forget about it. Don't let this get in your head. I think you're looking for an excuse to mess things up with him."

"You do?" I take a few seconds to think about that. "Oh, maybe that's part of it. Now, I have more questions than answers. You suck!"

"My advice is just don't go there with him. Date the cute boy, and have fun. You need to chill. So... let's go next door. It'll be so much more fun than whatever this is." Simone waves her index finger toward my laptop and backpack and then at my head.

I nod, wiping away the damp tears that have formed at the corner of my eyes. She's right.

I take her hand. "I agree. This is me chilling." I let out a deep breath. "Now, let's go try on some lipsticks."

* * *

BRANDON

Though we text a bunch on Sunday, I don't see Alli on Monday morning. Our school schedules are not lined up this semester. I need to make an effort for our paths to cross.

I know she has lunch while I have study hall, so I figure that gives me an opening.

I text her.

I'm going to the tutoring center to knock out my homework.
Can you stop by?

Ten minutes later, there is still no reply from her. I stop scrolling through Instagram and dig into my calculus worksheet.

Just as the class period is about to wrap up, I sense someone next to me.

"Hey, listen to this," Alli whispers in my ear as she gently sticks in an earbud. My body startles at the unexpected sensation. She has the other earbud tucked into her right ear as she bends toward the table in front of us, all smiles, and bumps me half off my chair. Then she fumbles with her phone for a minute and starts a video— "Remember I Told You" by Nick Jonas.

"I think I convinced Shea to add this to the playlist," she says proudly. "You know, she's on the prom committee."

Awkwardly, I balance on half a chair, smushed up against her, as the music plays in both our heads. Together, we watch Nick, Mike Posner, and Anne-Marie sing and dance inside a small white room, surrounded by a funky parade of people with amazing dance moves.

Just as the song winds down, the bell rings for the end of the period. She quickly spools the white cord around her phone and sticks both in her back jeans pocket.

"Cool, right?"

"Did you have to pay off Shea?" I ask as we pop up to standing. Everybody knows Alli has a rabid Nick Jonas obsession.

"Ha, ha. No. It's a great song."

"That happens to include Nick Jonas."

"Yeah, that, too." She waves a goodbye to Luca, who mans the front desk of the Tutoring Center.

"Haven't you been to a bunch of his concerts? Like a scary number of them?"

"Not a scary number, Brandon. Five is totally a normal number, considering I started going in sixth grade." Her tone is hyper-defensive. "I mean, some of the shows were the Jonas Brothers, not *just* him."

As we head down the hallway, Alli looks my way as though bracing for me to make further fun of her Jonas mania. I decide to let this sensitive topic go and brush my hand lightly against hers. She quickly accepts my gesture and wraps her fingers around mine. As we glide as one unit toward our seventh-period classes, I feel like I own the hallway.

I refuse to admit this to Alli, but I can't get that song out of my head for the rest of the day.

* * *

ALLI

Since my friends and I text constantly, and even my dad usually texts me before he calls, I'm taken by surprise when my phone rings while I'm chilling in the family room, watching *This Is Us* with my mom. I glance down and see Brandon's name on my screen.

"Mom, I'll be right back. You can keep it going and just fill me in."

"I did it. I quit the Dolphins." His tone is light and breezy.

"*Whaaat?*" I let his words sink in while I walk to the living room.

"I wanna enjoy my final months of high school and not be chained down. So, when I fucked up that last race, it just messed with my mind. I'm relieved, and I think Coach is, too. He even told me he was happy with my decision. He said, and I quote, 'I recognize your heart is no longer 150 percent committed to do what it takes to win.' Coach Cam is clairvoyant, what can I say?"

"Okay. Well, if that's what you need to do, then I'm happy for you," I say, as I pick the gray dog hairs off my red Miami University of Ohio sweatshirt, the school I'll be swimming for in six short months. "What did your parents say?"

"They are fine with it, but they want me to follow through on my commitments to the team out of the pool. So, I have to go to the awards dinner. Which is fine. I can manage that."

"That's good. Hey, my mom and I are watching a show. Can we talk more about things tomorrow? I'm glad you called, though. To tell me your news."

"Sure. Night, Alli. See you tomorrow," Brandon says as he hangs up.

As I walk back into the family room and sit down next to my mom, I admit to myself I'm a little bit jealous of his sudden freedom. I've always had a love-hate relationship with swimming. The second after my alarm buzzes at 5 a.m., my first thought, as I'm lying cozy under the covers is: *I HATE SWIMMING*. It's just the worst feeling in the world, trudging to Simone's car at 5:30 a.m. dressed head to toe against the bitter cold, then walking into a locker room only to emerge minutes later wearing a thin layer of nylon before diving into a 79-degree pool for 6 a.m. drills.

Then there's the chlorine that gives all us swimmers brittle hair; it's why I'm constantly pulling out my tube of moisturizer from my backpack, to try to keep alligator skin at bay. For extra measure, don't forget the grueling eight practices a week that include pool and strength training. During full-day meets, it means cycling in and out of the water, where the pool deck is either freezing or stiflingly humid. It's also why, about three times a year, I end up needing a prescription to treat "swimmer's ear."

Cam has been my club team head swim coach for the past six years. My dad signed me up when I was in sixth grade and scored a soccer goal for the other team then refused to put on cleats ever again. Right away, my dad and Cam seemed to bond.

My dad became the parent Coach Cam would pull up a chair next to whenever the team went out for meals on the road. One day, our teammate, Tyler, thinking he was being funny, pissed me off in front of a bunch of my seventh-grade teammates by asking if my dad and Cam were "gay friends."

"Why are you such an asshole?" Peter said, getting in his face and putting a hard stop to Tyler's big mouth.

Cam is married and would sometimes bring his five-year-old son to practice, so Tyler was just being an idiot, something he is still very good at. (Tyler had the worst bacne; I think he got pissed off at training and swim meets because everyone was seeing his gross back. It was pretty awful!)

It took me a while to understand what drew him to my dad. Cam competes in triathlons for fun and often tells us his favorite thing about triathlons is that he gets a whole day for himself. Seriously! His standard motivational locker room speech includes goodies like reminding us we shouldn't bother to get out of bed unless we plan to give 150 percent to what we are about to do in the pool.

I can see how Cam appreciates how, unlike some of the other parents, my dad cheers loudly from the sidelines at meets but never second-guesses his coaching decisions. I spend four months each fall swimming for the high school team, where I've had two different coaches, while for the other eight months each year, I swim for Cam on the Dolphins. He's the one who taught me how to break out of the pack.

It was halfway into my freshman year on the high school swim team when I started dropping time and got pulled up to varsity. At sectionals, I knew I would have to shave off a few tenths to place. When I looked up at the scoreboard and saw I had cut my time by .20 seconds, it was one of the happiest moments of my life. All the early mornings, the disappointments and setbacks just melted away. I had made it. I was going to State. That's the part I love!

* * *

BRANDON

My friend Jimmy has lived on the same block as me since our family moved into our white wood-framed house the summer before kindergarten. Luckily, he has a car he only has to give up on the handful of days when his twenty-two-year-old brother is in town from Colorado. I catch a ride with him to school on days I don't have to be there super-early for swim practice, which now is every day. I get that some of my swim teammates think it's a dick move. But at least Coach Cam isn't upset about my decision to literally throw in the towel. He saw my motivation was lacking. That I wasn't bringing my best into the pool these past few months. He's probably thrilled I'm opening the door for Emery, as his 200-free rivals mine, and he's only a sophomore.

Jimmy whips out of his front door, his short brown hair still wet, and claps me on the back hard with his palm. He doesn't realize that whacking someone when you are six-foot-two and two hundred pounds hurts, but I man up and ignore it. "Hey, did you hear about Ryan Peters?"

"Yeah, that he's going to West Point?"

"No, dumbass, that's Ryan G. Ryan P is the junior. He had some people over last night, and the paramedics had to show up because JoJo threw up all over the kitchen floor and then passed out. The cops came, but by then everyone had run out the back door except JoJo's best friend, Ella, who was freaking out and crying."

"That's fucking insane!"

"Oh, and listen to this. The parents were upstairs, totally clueless, so Ryan's mom comes down when she hears Ella losing it and ends up giving JoJo mouth-to-mouth while Ella calls 911."

I squelch a smile as the chaotic images flash in my mind. "Wow! Is JoJo okay?"

"The hospital had to pump her full of fluids for more than twenty-four hours. I guess she brought a water bottle full of vodka to Ryan's and was drinking it and passing it around."

"Man, that is fucked up. Coach Schrader is going to be mad as shit if he loses his star pitcher. The baseball team is so screwed without Ryan."

"Yeah, but doesn't Ella swim with Alli? She's in trouble, too."

"Seriously? She was drinking? Cam is going to be pissed as hell. Ella's the top relay finisher. I have to text Alli."

I jump into Jimmy's red Ford Explorer, and as soon as he turns on the ignition, music explodes from the speakers. Jimmy's got the best musical taste, because it crosses all genres. He loves music in every form, and I rarely push the thumbs-down button on his choices, even though he has an obsession with Pearl Jam songs from every decade.

Wanting to hear myself think, I turn the volume down on Two Feet's new release, "I Feel Like I'm Drowning," though we blasted it full-on when we first listened to it yesterday. I start a texting chain with Alli that is fast and furious. I tell her what I know, and she fills in a few details she got from one of her group texts (police were there for a whole hour, asking questions; Ella is JoJo's girlfriend), until we piece together this whole messy story. Bottom line: it is only going to mean bad news for Ryan, JoJo, and Ella.

"They all could lose their driver's licenses, and that is just the start of all the shit that's going to go down," I tell Jimmy, as Alli and I take a break from our frenzied texting. "They have a meeting with the principal and their parents this week."

"All I know is I have a few more months and then, none of this matters. College, baby!" Jimmy pounds the steering wheel with his fist.

His words put my brain into worry mode, on top of this shitstorm of a story. Jimmy is going to U. of Illinois. He's even got his roommate all worked out.

Wisconsin is the school I really want to go to. So far, I'm in at my one safety school, and that's it. It's all hanging on an email from them telling me I'm in the door.

* * *

ALLI

I'm super excited the third part of one of my favorite book series, *Maze Runner*, is going to be in theatres this weekend. I decide to drag

Brandon to it, even though the first two movies weren't as good as the novels. They never are, I guess. Still, I need to see how it all ends up. I text Brandon.

> *The Maze Runner movie comes out this week.*

> *Yeah, I saw the first one. Just OK.*

> *I'll fill you in on what you missed. Loved the books, have to see it through.*

> *Let's go. What time?*

> *Early. I have a winter invitational, so I'll be beat. 5:30 movie?*

> 👍 *I'm sleeping 'til noon.*

I text him the middle finger emoji, because that's just mean, although I would do the same if I could.

Brandon told me he's convinced he never wants to see a swimming pool again. I can't imagine how he could quit swimming cold turkey. Swimming gets into your blood, brain, cells, and heart. Or is that just me?

It's 5:30 a.m., and I'm in the passenger seat next to my slightly scruffy-looking dad. It's a bit jarring, as he's always clean-shaven, even when I have a super-early meet. As he drives, he tries to hide his third yawn in about five minutes, so I decide not to tease him about his gray-and-brown stubble. He obviously had a late night. Dad's got on the baggy blue Dolphin sweats I got him for Father's Day my freshman year. They look a little less baggy now. The few pounds that have creeped on these past few years and the gray hair that now mixes in with his short, brown curls give him a maturity that, in my humble opinion, works for him, though that was before he showed up this morning with whiskers.

We're headed a few towns away to a sectional meet, with winners qualifying for State. During these car rides, Dad always wears his coaching hat. My dad is no athlete. And he's never been more than a recreational swimmer. But he made it his mission to study up on competitive swimming. He became a master of swim speak, and completely gets the meanings behind DPS, RI, smooth, zoomers, recovery, pre-set, warm-down. He is passionate about every tiny timing detail and recognizes the value in every important and not-so-important set I complete in practice drills.

"How many days did you plan to take off this year after short-course season?" Dad asks as we turn into the parking lot of the massive brick high school that's hosting our swim meet. The radio is off, as it always is when Dad takes me to a competition. He wants to make sure I stay focused and "clear my head."

Chase, who rocks the 100-meter butterfly, will be my only friend at the meet today. He'll be swimming for Penn State in the fall. Most of my senior swim team friends take a break after short-course season or, more likely, hang it up for good and enjoy the rest of senior year swim-free.

"I'll just drop the week of spring break. But I'll be ready for long-course. I've been killing it with my timing on turns."

"Well, for today, there's that sophomore to watch out for, Lindsey from Central," Dad warns, parking the car. "Cam says she's on fire right now."

"I am too, though, Dad. Just you watch." Honestly, I wish I could have flipped on some tunes and chilled out on the way over here. The mood in this car is too intense for so early in the morning.

As I head into the locker room, I mentally prepare for Cam's pre-meet warm-up in the pool, which is followed by a five-minute dry-land circuit and stretching. When I step onto the pool deck in my navy-blue swimsuit with the dolphin logo, my skin is hit by the chill air all around me. Goosebumps erupt along my arms as I walk to the first lane and dive in from the deep end.

Immediately, shock registers as the chilly pool waters envelop me. I start my strokes, but I'm not happy that the deck and pool temperatures are both so shockingly cold. Heading for my first flip turn, I tuck my knees in tight and somersault through the water. I push off hard from the wall to distract myself from the polar conditions I've plunged into headfirst.

PRE-MEET WARM-UP 6 a.m. to 6:30 a.m.

600 Freestyle

400 IM Kick/Drill

3 x 100 IM Swim

4 x 50 Fast/Easy/Fast

100 Easy

As I shift from breast into fly, I take a two-second break at the pool's edge and scope out my dad. I find him exactly where I expected: in the first row of bleachers, Nikon video cam in hand, talking to another swim parent. Since I started competitive swimming, he's videotaped every race I've competed in. He's constantly posting action photos from my meets behind the register in his shop and will tell any customer who asks about his daughter's swimming prowess.

I couldn't have gotten a free ride to Miami-Ohio without him having my back.

Driving home after the meet, Dad and I dissect my missed opportunities, the tough competition, and the subpar meet conditions that led to a disappointing finish in two of the four races I swam today. I usually dread our post-meet car rides, but now I actively tune into his advice. I use this time to go over my performance and talk out where things went wrong.

When we're blocks from my house, I pull my phone from my swim bag. "Hey, Dad, I'm seeing a movie later, *Maze Runner*. The third one is out."

"Yeah? I remember seeing the first one with you when you were a freshman. Do you think you should be going to a movie tonight? You need to be on top of your game tomorrow."

You think I should stay home all night?" I hear my voice launching into whine-mode, which I know he hates. "I'll just watch a stupid movie, so I might as well go out and do that. I'm still gonna sleep 'til noon." This makes complete sense to me, even though I am sure my dad and Coach Cam would disagree. "Since I don't have to check in to the finals tomorrow until 3, I want to try to see the later movie," I add. Dad can be such a drag. I mean should I really have to defend my desire to be social? Or not stay cooped up at home with my eight-year-old brothers on a Saturday night?

My thumbs type quickly on the screen.

Can we see 8 pm movie?

"Say hi to Simone for me," Dad says, his voice tighter than usual.

"Oh, I'm going with Brandon, not Simone. He's on the club team, too. Well, he was. He just quit. You'll meet him at the senior swim dinner in April," I say before stopping to take a breath.

"But if he quit the team, why's he going to that?"

"He promised his mom. She's ex-Marine. A real hard-ass," I explain.

"Got it," he says, turning onto my street.

My phone buzzes, a glowing message back from Brandon.

OK. I'll get you at 7:30.

"I've seen Brandon swim," Dad says after I drop my phone back in my bag. "The 200. He's not bad. Why'd he quit?"

"His lost his mojo."

Dad nods his head as he pulls into my driveway and puts the car in park. We've seen it all from the sidelines, the revolving door of swim faces.

"I look forward to meeting him then," he says, softening his tone, before we both step out of the car. "I'll pick you up tomorrow at, say, 2:30." He hugs me tightly and kisses my forehead before letting me free.

"Sure, Dad. I'll be ready," I grab my swim bag and head up my front walk, fixating on the nap I plan to take in about fifteen minutes.

* * *

BRANDON

I walked Astor and downed a turkey sandwich all before 7 p.m. I want to make sure I'm on time today to pick up Alli for a movie she's excited to see. I'm just excited to see her.

"Your brothers are adorable," I say as we shut the front door to her house after I meet the whole family. "It's funny how Sammy's got dark hair like yours and Tommy's is much lighter. I wouldn't have guessed they are twins."

"Yeah, I agree. It is pretty great, because they don't have to worry about people confusing them with each other. That would suck to be called your brother's name all the time. They do look really alike in a lot of other ways," Alli adds. "Is it mean how I love that my mom, brothers, and I all have the exact same greenish-brown eyes, while Ray's are just plain-old gray?"

I shake my head and massage my right hand as we walk down her front steps toward my car. "When your stepdad shook my hand, I thought he was going to pull it off," I say as we settle into our seats.

"Yeah, sorry. He's kind of a jerk," Alli says.

I study my extended fingers for a permanent red mark from his grip then grab the steering wheel to drive us to the movie theater. Luckily, there's no discoloration. Just a radiating pain that starts to travel up my arm.

"I don't think he did it on purpose," I add, not wanting to start the night off with a bad vibe.

"Or *did* he?" she says in her most sinister voice. "I'm just annoyed because, earlier today, my mom tells me next weekend Ray's dad is having a seventy-fifth birthday party. She asked me if I was okay staying home to watch the dog while they take my brothers overnight to Iowa."

"Really? That's what she said?"

"Well no, it's more passive-aggressive than that. It's, like, I know you're busy with swimming and want to be with your friends. Which is true. I really don't want to go sit around with a bunch of Ray's relatives. But I still would have liked to have been asked first, you know?"

"Yeah, that is pretty shitty." I look over at her and our eyes meet for a split-second of solidarity. I want her to know she can always be brutally honest with me. Especially when her mom and stepdad make her crazy. "My parents are the opposite actually," I confess. "They just assume I want to do all these boring things with them. A typical Friday night is spent with the History Channel playing, though I often find them sleeping in front of the TV more than watching it."

Alli laughs loudly. "Thanks. I needed that," she says, smiling at me. "Hey, did you hear any updates about Ella and Ryan's meeting with the principal?"

"I just heard they all have to do, like, twenty-five hours of community service, but they got so lucky. They only got warning tickets, so they don't have to go in front of a judge or anything like that. Though I think Ryan and Ella are both sidelined for a whole season—I'm not sure."

"That sucks so bad for them. I hope they can work it out. Did you know a junior who got busted vaping in the lunchroom last year joined the soccer team in the fall and sat on the sidelines all season, just so he could get his sports-season punishment out of the way? Then he went back to volleyball in the winter. Maybe they can do something like that."

"That seems weird, but I guess it could happen. Anyway, how did the meet go?" I ask hopefully. "Did you make State?"

"I was a little off my best. Remember that tall sophomore from Central? She was totally destroying it. She won every race by body lengths." She sighs, adding, "I had no chance in the 100 or 200 free, but I got a PR in the 200 medley and was off my PR in the 100 fly by half a second."

"That sucks, when these swimmers come up and just crush it, but qualifying in two events is still really strong. How was your dad on the car ride home?" She's told me how he can be a pain in the ass when Alli falters in competition.

"He was pretty low-key today. He did say he was bummed I didn't push myself too much in the warmup. The water was so cold, and I didn't want my muscles to freeze up, you know? He doesn't get how much that really matters."

"Of course, it matters!" I say. I think of the many times I've been in that situation. "Sounds like you did everything you could."

"I did. And now what I need is to zone out to a creepy movie. Aren't you psyched?" she asks with a wicked smile. She knows I'm not.

I pull the car into a parking space a half block from the movie theater. Turning to Alli before we climb out of the car, I admit, "Psyched isn't the word I'd choose."

We walk up to the glass ticket window, and when I study the movie start times, I try not to notice that *12 Strong*, about the first Special Forces team deployed to Afghanistan after 9/11, just came out, too. I need to see that super-soon.

"Two tickets to *Maze Runner*," I say to the young girl behind the window. She sports a tiny diamond stud in her nose and blue-tinged hair in floppy pigtails, a style choice I find a bit confusing. I pass over a $20 bill and pick up our two movie tickets and my change, then I turn to take Alli's hand in mine.

"Let's get some popcorn," she says, leading us inside the theater as she pulls a $10 bill from her front jeans pocket. "An extra-large one, because I'm hungry."

Now we're talking!

* * *

ALLI

"Cam was brutal today," Simone says, stating the obvious, as we slam our lockers shut after we've showered and changed back into our clothes. "Do you want to grab Starbucks on the way home?"

"I have too much homework. Raincheck?" I say as we walk outside to her car. "Did I tell you my mom and Ray are taking my brothers to Iowa this weekend?"

"No. Are you having a party Saturday night?" she asks. "I definitely will be there with Darryl."

"Simone," I respond, tightly grasping her forearm to stop her in her tracks. "I'm not thinking party. I'm thinking me and Brandon hanging out."

She turns to me with a sly smile. "Oh. Well, good for you. Finally, you and Brandon. It's perfect. You two together."

"I'm pretty nervous about it all. Shouldn't I be?"

"Oh my, Alli. Losing it to Brandon. Does it feel right?"

"I think so. Should I feel more sure than that?"

"Well, do you believe he's the right person for you? For this?"

I nod. We squeeze hands and continue walking to the car, Simone pulling me along.

"Does your mom know about you and Brandon?" she asks.

"He made this big show about picking me up before the movie last week, so he met Mom and Ray then, and also my little brothers. I think it's obvious we're dating. She hasn't really pried about it. She did say she thinks he's 'cute' and 'seems nice,'" I say, making air quotes.

"Well, if she's not telling you to be careful, I will," she says seriously.

"Simone!"

"Yeah, sorry. What was I thinking? You're the most together person I know."

"Ha. Then you need to get out more." I laugh as we both lower ourselves into her car's bucket seats.

* * *

FEBRUARY 10

BRANDON

When I woke up this morning, I decided I needed to ask Alli to prom, to kick our night off right. And then I had my epiphany. Kick... kickboard... prom. This afternoon, I went to two Targets before finally finding what I needed at the Play It Again Sports resale store thirty minutes away.

The sky is fading to black as I pull my mom's car into Alli's driveway and park, the much sought-after kickboard lying beside me in the passenger seat.

I ring her doorbell feeling stupid, excited, nervous. Stupid because I'm holding the blue kickboard; excited because, well, I'm hanging with my girlfriend. Nervous because her family is out of town. That means anything and everything can happen. I want everything to happen, and I think Alli does, too.

She throws the door open wide, smiling at me with a questioning look as her eyes fall on the kickboard. She's wearing black leggings and a slightly oversized black shirt with a Nike swoosh in one corner. I immediately feel overdressed in dark jeans and green long-sleeve Polo under my coat.

"C'mon, let's go swimming," I say, pushing our attire out of my mind to focus on my promposal.

"Um, okay. This is weird," she says, leaning against the door frame.

"Why? We totally should go swimming." I know I make no sense. But I have to roll with the game I'm playing.

"Brandon, what's going on?" she asks, finally hip to the fact I'm pulling her leg.

I turn the kickboard on its side and then flip it over, where I've written the words *Kick it at PROM?* in big, block letters with Sharpie. I hand it over to her.

"So? What do you think?"

She accepts my gift and reads the carefully written text for a long, drawn-out minute. She then hits me over the head with the foam board.

"You're a nut," she says. "But prom is months away. Isn't this a little early to decide? We may hate each other by then."

"Alli, you know I've liked you since forever. And the more I get to know you, the more I really like you." I put *all* my cards on the table, and now I'm nervous. I didn't think about the other side of things. Like, if she says a polite, "No, but thanks for asking." Or, "Maybe." Or even a straight-out, "No." I just went with my gut and showed up on her doorstep hopeful and impulsive.

She studies the words on the foam board again for a few more agonizing seconds and then smiles up at me. "Sure. I'd love to go to prom with you."

"Great," I respond with a sigh of relief. "We're going to have a blast." I rub the spot where the board made contact with my head. "It's a good thing I haven't had my hair cut in a while, or that could have killed some of my brain cells."

"Lucky me. You definitely don't have any to spare," she says, moving out of the way as I sweep past her into the living room. "I made cookies. Do you want some?"

She takes my coat and hangs it up on the coatrack in the front hall. Then I follow her into the kitchen and sit down at the white round table pushed up against one wall of the totally white room. At first, it's jarring to be in a room where every surface is white—the counters, the cabinets, the square-tile floor. There is some colorful kid artwork, though, that's taped on the white walls and completely covers the fridge. A large window over the sink frames the dark night outside so that the kitchen feels clean and bright.

She sets down a plate and I grab a cookie.

"Whoa, it's warm." I swallow it in three bites and grab for a second.

She shrugs as she sits next to me and picks up a large, slightly misshapen cookie. "They're just from a mix." She breaks it in half and hands one part to me. "I've already had one. Well, two."

"Now we're both at two and a half." I accept her offering and pop it in my mouth. "We're tied."

She grabs a bottle of lemonade from the fridge and pours two generous glassfuls. She brings them to the table before sitting back in her chair.

"So, what should we do?" I ask, after draining my glass. I want to see what's on Alli's agenda for our evening.

"Well, maybe Jenga?"

"Sweet, but I have to warn you. You're going down." I'm not that great at Jenga, but my one rule in any competition is to always psych out the opponent. Even the one you're dating. I briefly wonder if I should reconsider that ground rule... *Naw!*

We move into the family room, where I flop onto the floor in front of a square, wooden coffee table. Alli grabs the orange box from a cabinet and hands it to me as she sits. Our knees fuse for a minute, before she shifts slightly away. We start to stack the Jenga tower, our fingers touching as we alternate putting the small, wood blocks into the set-up tray in the middle of the table.

Six moves into our game, I pull out a block and the structure comes crashing down.

"Brandon! You are so not the Jenga master," she says, laughing.

I lean over her to brush away a few of the blocks that landed near her legs. She looks at me with eyes that just slay my heart.

I maneuver my head so it's inches from her face and lean in to kiss her lips deeply. Her tongue impatiently finds mine. Soon, we are making out in the midst of a Jenga pile.

She pulls back from me gently and picks up a block. As she occupies her hands, putting away the game pieces, she says softly, "It's my first time. You know that, right?"

I nod. "You want this to happen?"

"Yes, I do. I trust you."

"We'll go slow. I— want what's good for you," I stammer.

"I know," she says. "You have...?" She pauses, letting the next word hang out there unsaid but definitely understood.

"Yes. In my pocket." I stand up and pat the condom I shoved in there before leaving my house.

She looks at me seriously for a long minute before taking my outstretched hand and standing beside me. Our hands stay locked together as we head up the stairs and down the hallway lined with framed family photos. I step into her bedroom just behind her, and she slowly turns to face me. Alli tiptoes closer to me, and we fall sloppily onto her twin bed. Our lips and legs and arms tangle together. I kiss her hungrily, eagerly.

* * *

ALLI

I slow us down. There's no rush to get where we are going. I want to enjoy making out with this cute boy in my room, on my bed. I'm in no hurry to get to the unfamiliar part of this night.

I realize it's going to hurt. Simone told me to expect it to hurt. Knowing that makes it hard to completely relax. So, it's good that Brandon is such an amazing kisser. I'm distracted by his warm, caressing lips as they move down my neck and across my chest.

I stand in front of the washing machine, spraying Shout on the bloodstain. I didn't expect there to be this much blood. As I shove the sheets into the washing machine, I think of the memories I have in my room. Kid memories: lying sick, tucked tightly under the sheets, as my mom brought me cinnamon toast and orange juice; propped up in bed at 1 a.m. or 11 a.m. or anytime, actually, with my computer on my stomach, doing homework or watching a movie or YouTube video.

Now, my bed, these sheets, will never feel the same. And I feel different, too. Raw and tender after what we just did together. At the same time, lit up from the inside.

I walk out of the laundry room just off the kitchen and find Brandon in the family room, rooting around for the TV remote.

I lean under the coffee table and grab for the channel changer on a little shelf.

"Is this what you need?" I ask, holding it close to my chest.

Brandon nods his head up and down with a silly smile on his face before he drops onto the cushy blue sofa.

"How are you?" he asks tenderly, carefully. "Do you feel okay?"

"I feel more than okay, Brandon," I say. "I feel kinda great."

"We are kinda great together. That's why I wanted to ask you to prom tonight. So you know I'm serious about us."

How does he always say just what I want to hear? How does he know me, know my heart so well?

I collapse onto the sofa cushions next to him, turn on the TV, and flip around the channels.

"What should we watch?" I ask as I land on the Food Network. "*Chopped Junior* is Kaitlyn's favorite show. She's got the whole team hooked. When we have away meets, we only watch that or *MasterChef Junior* while we zone out in our hotel rooms."

"Uh, no thanks," Brandon replies. "Let's check out Netflix."

"We don't have it. My stepdad is not a fan. He thinks we have enough choices without it."

"No Netflix. You really are deprived," he jokes. "Have you ever seen *The Amazing Race*?"

"Oh, that's the show where teams have to follow an insane scavenger hunt? Never seen it."

"Well, I've watched every episode. My buddy Matt and I are going to be on it one day. We're going to win, too." He grins.

"Um, good luck with that. You would be hilarious together."

"It doesn't sound like you think we could be conquering *champions*," Brandon says, loudly emphasizing the last word and raising his hands above his head in mock triumph.

"Sorry to burst your bubble. Matt is really smart and all, but I am not sure he could handle the pressure. Remember when he texted that his dog Shaggy got out of the house and asked all of us to help look for him?"

"Yeah, that was funny. We're all driving around town searching for his dog for hours when it was sleeping in his basement the whole time."

I speak into the remote, and his show pops up. I hand the controls over to Brandon, and he scrolls through the episodes.

"Can we watch this one?" he asks when a recent episode comes on. "I think you'll really like it."

"Sure, Brandon." I lean my head against his shoulder. "I'm game."

* * *

BRANDON

Alli and I watch two episodes of *The Amazing Race*. I think she's hooked on it, too. It was her idea to binge watch. I was even going to cave and check out the Food Channel with her, after the first episode ended.

After the shows, we put her dog Murphy on a leash and walk him to the corner, so he can do his business. He's an old, grumpy, squat, hotdog-looking thing with zero dog appeal.

"I know you can't tell, because he's twelve years old," Alli explains, "but this dog used to walk around our house all day with a huge grungy bone in his mouth, wanting to play."

"Well, that is true. You wouldn't know it now." The scrawny, slow-moving gray mop of curly hair glares up at me, his eyes poking out and his tail playing dead.

Alli and I share a lingering kiss goodnight, and then I head out to the car. I have a lot to be happy about. Alli and I are solid, and we are going to have such an epic time at prom. I didn't even tell her the post-prom deal yet. Matt's uncle has a house on the lake in Wisconsin with canoes and an outdoor fire pit. His twenty-five-year-old cousin, Lucy, is going to stay there, too, so all the parents can relax about us being up there for the weekend.

* * *

ALLI

I stand in the living room, peering out the front window for my dad's car, when my back pocket buzzes with a new text alert.

>*Simone: Just got back from my cousin's baby shower in Indiana.*

Alli: Fun?

>*Kinda. She's having a boy. Boy clothes so BORING.*

Still. That's exciting. Happy 4 her.

>*SO??*

Yes?

>*So... did you?*

Yes!

>*AND???*

>*AND???*

>*FINE! IU2U.*

BFN. Going to dinner with dad.

>*Enjoy Olive Garden.* 😊

I shove the phone back in my jeans pocket and focus out the window again. Every Sunday night at 6 p.m., Dad picks me up and we grab dinner, usually Italian. Both my parents have Sicilian moms, so I am used to dining frequently on combinations of pasta, cheese, and meat.

I try to be there for my dad like he has always been here for me. I just hope that's enough. Soon, I will be three hundred miles away, living wall-to-wall with masses of teenagers in a college dorm, and I already worry that, between the two of us, he may have the hardest adjustment.

When I spend time with each of my parents, I live in two different worlds. My mom has it all... the house and husband and family. And you know what my dad has... me and his shop. He has made it clear every day that my dreams, my passions, are his number-one priority. Which makes it pretty hard for mom and Ray to step up, considering their energy and focus is obviously, and I get it, my whirlwind twin brothers.

For the past five years, my dad and I have been a team, working toward a singular goal: to get me a college scholarship.

Part of my parents' divorce agreement was that my dad is supposed to contribute to my "post-high school educational expenses," but I know the pawnshop doesn't throw off the cash to make a dent in any future tuition bills. On top of that, while my mom works part-time as the district sales manager for an appliance company and has said she would "help out," my village-planner stepdad has made it clear he isn't so keen on footing my college bills.

I was game for the challenge, for the freedom it promised. Once I fell in love with swimming and realized I was good at it, I was all in. We never asked my coach if I would land a free ride. It was *how*. It was, "Tell us, Cam, what would it take?"

Cam taught me how to master my starts, nail my turns, and finish strong. No matter if I am feeling sick, tired, or just lazy, he pushes me to stay single-minded. I learned to race hard any time and against anyone with no excuses because, with Cam, there are none.

Almost every freaking day of the year since I was thirteen, I've been in a pool. Cam told me, if I stayed the course, perfecting my freestyle strokes and times, I'd have college swim coaches knocking at my door. And you know what? He was right.

Because of my dad and Cam, I'm going to college without being a burden to my family with bills they can't afford.

As I think about how our weekly dinners are one tradition we will need to let go of soon, he pulls into the driveway. I know how much my dad hates ringing the doorbell here, and I don't blame him, so I try to always be ready and watch for his arrival.

We meet outside his car door for a tight hug and begin our Sunday night routine.

"Hi, Dad. What's up?"

"My appetite," he jokes for the ten thousandth time. "I need bread and cheese."

"Italian is fine. But not Olive Garden, please. I eat too many breadsticks there."

As we slide into the booth at Mario's, each of us picks up our laminated menu. Dad pats his paunchy stomach. "Everything you see I owe to spaghetti." He laughs at the latest cheesy one-liner he has stolen from some famous actor.

"You can do something about that," I remind him. Dad used to coach my Little League teams when I was in elementary school, first softball and then club soccer, but once I found swimming, he moved over to the sidelines.

"I know," he says. "And I should. I have a fourth date next weekend with Padma."

"Padma? I like that name. It's different."

"She's great. I've known her a while. She owns a store on Devon that sells Indian saris and jewelry. She comes into the pawnshop once in a while to check out our gold. One day last month, I got this amazing gold bracelet in trade and met her for coffee to show it to her. We talked for three hours. She's been divorced for a long time, too, and has a fifteen-year-old son, Shobin, and a daughter, Rina, who's studying costume design at the Art Institute."

I look up from my menu. His face is lit up with a magical glow I've never seen before, not even when he relishes my State race results.

Dad telling me about his love life. This is a first. Maybe he will be okay without me around.

* * *

FEBRUARY 14

BRANDON

"I asked Alli to prom Saturday night," I tell Jimmy as I jump into his car twenty minutes before the first period bell. I promised myself I wouldn't tell anybody yet. But today, I am not my normal self. It's the first Valentine's Day where I feel completely and deeply crazy about someone. An amazing someone.

"Seriously? Why the rush? I mean, you just started dating." He glances at me like I have two heads and then whips his eyes back to the road.

"But we've known each other for a long time," I explain. "I just wanted her to know this is not a fling."

"Well, I'm not going to think about prom yet. I have Valentine's Day to worry about today."

"True! Are you sending anyone a singing Valentine? Shelby?"

"Ha, no way. That is not my thing. Did you shell out for that? It's just a school choir scam."

"Last year, Darcy sent me one when I was in Spanish, and it was so embarrassing. I promised myself I would never do that to anyone."

As we drive, Shelby's name appears on Jimmy phone as it rings. He hits a button to answer, and the call blares out via his car's Bluetooth.

"So, I just got a great financial aid package from American," she begins. I try to fade into the background as they talk about her good news. I think about what Jimmy just said. He just doesn't get how my connection with Alli may seem new, but it really goes way back.

She is actually one of the reasons I went out for the high school swim team and then took up club swimming. When I didn't make the cut from thirty-five guys to the twenty-two on the roster for the high school soccer team in the fall of freshman year, I alternated from being completely bummed to royally pissed off at the coach who'd passed me over. He tried to justify it, saying he "had too many strong offensive players to choose from," which only further battered my ego. *Then why did Jack and Quintin make the cut?* I'd easily schooled them a bunch of times on the field when we played club soccer together in middle school.

After a few weeks of "poor me," I picked myself up, dusted myself off, and decided to embrace a new challenge. Every summer since I was eight, I'd been on the swim team at our town's swim and racquet club and never embarrassed myself. I figured, in swimming, at least I'd get to hang around cute girls in bathing suits, Alli included. How hard could it be to jump back into the swim of things, this time with the high school team?

Insane hard was the answer. Swimming is one of the few sports at our school where we have two practices a day, a strength workout twice a week before school, something called dry-land training, and then two hours in the pool after school. Oh, and three hours on Saturdays. There's nothing more brutal than setting an alarm for Saturday morning at 5 a.m.

Really quickly, swimming laps for hours turned my abs into six packs, and I became a pretty damn good anchor for the 200-yard freestyle relay.

The bathing suit strategy worked out pretty well, too. Hey, don't write me off as a male chauvinist pig. I've seen the girl swimmers do the same thing to us guys.

"So, Brandon's in the car, too," Jimmy announces to Shelby after she finishes sharing her news.

"Hey, that's a big deal about American," I say. "D.C. is a cool town."

"Yeah, thanks. Did you hear about Wisconsin yet?"

"I'm still waiting."

"Well, good luck. Hey, I gotta go," she says and then clicks off.

"I hate to admit my sister was right," I tell Jimmy. "I should have applied by November 1, 'cuz I'd know by now."

Not only did my parents meet at Wisconsin in ROTC (BTW, that stands for Reserve Officers' Training Corps), but my sister is a junior there and loves everything about it. She's not a sports fan, except when it comes to Badgers football. Then she's dressed in red, pregaming on every game day, both home and away, and partying at tailgates. She even shows up in the stadium's student section for a few quarters, when the weather isn't freezing or raining.

"I think I purposely waited until almost the last date to apply, because Kelly and my mom were being so obsessive about it," I add.

"Well, that was kinda dumb of you," Jimmy says, piling on.

"Hey! I thought you were my friend."

"Seriously? What should I say? Congrats for procrastinating?"

"That would be better, yes. Alli's known she's going to Miami-Ohio since the summer. How lucky is that? She didn't even have to play the whole ridiculous application game."

"With her, it's not luck, though," he says. "I mean she did come in third at State last year."

"What's up with you today anyway? I'm the one dating her."

"Yeah, but I'm allowed to tell you when you're being an ass. Alli did play the game. She just played it on a different field than we did."

"I didn't know you'd joined the Alli fan club." I'm annoyed he's being a better friend to her than I'm being right now.

"I've always been a member, bro. I asked her to the homecoming dance sophomore year, before she started dating that brainiac, Ricardo, but she turned me down flat. I guess you're more her type."

"You got that right at least!" Jimmy has always been a bit of a player and likes to brag how girls tell him he looks like Shawn Mendes. I'm just glad Alli was immune to his charm. "How come you never told me you asked her out?"

Jimmy shrugs. He must realize he threw me a curveball. He parks the car, and we both jump out quickly. We're cutting it close to the bell. Our lockers are on opposite sides of the building, so we head in different directions.

"See ya," he says, pulling his phone out as he walks away.

I stare at my friend warily. "Later."

I want to be pissed about his confession about how he'd been crushing on Alli and decided this was the best time to tell me about it. But then I think about it. Who's the one she's going to prom with? I know it's not cool to gloat like I've won or something, but, well, I did totally win.

I pick up my pace, hoping to surprise Alli outside her first class and wish her a Happy Valentine's Day. I have a present for her on the dresser in my bedroom and a plan to invite her over after school to hang out and open it in private.

* * *

ALLI

Simone, no singing Valentines today PLEASE

I text her immediately after I rush in the high school front entrance, where I got a flyer thrust into my hand by a choir student dressed in red jeans, a white sweater with a red heart in the center, and *huge*, red, heart earrings flouncing above her shoulders.

A flurry of bodies flows through the busy hallway. Red, pink, and purple blotches of color float alongside red carnations, all coming at me from every direction. I fit in, though, in my red top with three white buttons trailing below my collarbone. This year, I am feeling—okay, embracing the Valentine's vibe.

As I hang up my puffy coat, Simone rushes up to my locker with a bag of Hershey's Kisses.

"I did shell out for a singing Valentine…," she announces.

I shake my head and am about to tell her how annoyed I am, but then she continues.

"…For Daryll. Don't worry! How about a Kiss?" She stuffs her hand in the bag and plucks out a silver-wrapped chocolate candy, dangling it from its paper stem.

I grab it. She's wearing black leggings dotted with red and purple hearts and—no surprise—her purple top with ruffles at the sleeves.

"Your favorite day!" I proclaim, as I eagerly unwrap the chocolate and pop it in my mouth.

"You know what is *so* funny, though?" She practically squeals with delight. "I see some teachers and then Jenna and Dylan all walking around with ash on their forehead, so I was like super-confused, at first. I thought maybe Valentine's Day was getting weird on me... But then I got it! Today's Ash Wednesday, too."

"Ha. That's awesome! I haven't seen that yet. Mr. Sullivan taught us last year with a big black cross on his forehead, and it was totally distracting, at first, but then I just got used to it."

The wall clock ticks down the last three minutes to first bell.

"Love you!" Simone says, as she grabs a few chocolates from the bag and presses them into my palm before sprinting down the hall to what she admits is her favorite class, AP US government.

I so run with the nerd herd.

I unwrap another candy and savor it as it melts slowly on my tongue. As I round the corner to graphic arts, I see Brandon waiting outside my classroom door, watching for my arrival.

"Hey," he says, pulling me close and surprising me with a short, sweet kiss. "I wanted to wish you a Happy Valentine's Day." He steps back after sampling my early morning treat. "*Mmm*... Chocolate."

"Here." I drop the two remaining Kisses into his hand. "There's more where that came from." As soon as the words are out of my mouth, I cringe. "Wow, that sounded slutty," I add, embarrassed. "I just meant, you know, Simone's got more chocolate."

He grins at my bumbling about. "I understand what you meant, Alli," he says diplomatically. "Hey, I'm going to be late. See you after school. I'll meet you near the front entrance." And he rushes toward the stairs for AP Calc.

My dad bugged me to add computer coding to my final-semester schedule. And after six weeks of class, I have learned a lot about computers, including the fact that coding is not for me. But Mr. Evers is a cool guy, and I've picked up enough to brag that "I can speak Python." I'm happy programming Hangman and Roll the Dice when I'm not tearing my hair out by having to stand up in front of the whiteboard and share some string of code I've written, as well as where it went right and wrong.

Seventh period is computer programming, so I'm plugged in when my phone starts to buzz. We are supposed to ignore our phones in class, and I usually do, but, as we all know, boredom leads to excessive phone scrolling.

> *Deputies are responding to reports of a shooting at Stoneman Douglas High. There are reports of victims. Shooter at large.*

I look around me. Everyone's typing furiously, working on their coding project and identifying infinite loops like nothing's different. "*HELLO?*" I want to scream. Am I the only one who knows this?

I scan the room. Is everyone so focused on our assignment, they don't register this? I want to will this headline away. To unknow this.

My heart races. My mind races. I sit in a stupor and stew silently, as I watch the clock tick down four minutes until the bell rings, and I am free from this room where everybody seems to be clueless about another shooting. At a high school.

Did people die? Students? Teachers? The shooter? Seniors like me? Freshmen at the beginning of their high school journey?

At the first sound of the bell, I log out of the school computer, grab my backpack, and hurry into the hallway. Business as usual. Everybody's rushing to their next class. Gabi passes by me, another senior I've known since kindergarten. I pull her aside.

"Hey, did you hear there is some shooting in Florida? At a school?"

She stares at me and shakes her head. We're so close, my nose starts to tickle from her long, blonde hair that whips from side to side. "Nope," she says. "That's fucked up. Let me see what you're talking about." She starts scrolling on her phone as she walks on to her next class.

I trudge up the stairs to eighth-period AP psych, walk into the room, and fling myself into my seat. "Hey!" I announce to no one. To everyone. "There's some school shooting that just happened."

"Yeah, I saw that," says Rori.

"Where?" asks Ian.

"Somewhere in Florida?" Rori explains.

"Who got shot? Like kids? What school?" Marlon asks rapid-fire, as he pulls out his phone.

"I don't think that's all been reported yet," I say, adding, "But high school students got shot."

I peer down at my phone. The newest headline.

Broward Sheriff's Office confirms there has been a shooting at Marjory Stoneman Douglas High School in Parkland, Florida. The school is currently on lockdown.

"Okay, class, settle down," says our teacher, Mr. Hale. "Let's all pull out the stress and health handout I passed out yesterday for discussion."

So, this is how it's going to be. Out of sight. Out of mind. As he drones on about approaches to stress (flight or fight, approach or avoidance), my thoughts jumble together in my head.

Am I safe here? If a gunman can come into my dad's shop, can come into a school and shoot it up, what security do I have that it can't happen here, won't happen to me or someone else I know?

I can't fight, but I also can't engage in flight. There's no approach, no avoidance. Just overwhelming, panicking, all-out stress. I think back to the dozens of mind-numbing times since kindergarten I've been in lockdown mode—crowded tightly on the floor with my classmates, all of us sitting knee-to-knee in a corner of the room, lights off, phones off, door locked and barricaded by desks, window blinds shut, and our teacher crouched alongside us nearest the door. Sitting ducks. Waiting for an all-clear signal, so we can resume our lessons while we pretend like nothing traumatic just happened.

Finally, class ends. I can recall nothing of what was said or shared or what I need to do about any of it. But I don't care. *Why should I? Why does any of this matter today? Tomorrow?*

Numb, I walk to my locker to grab my coat and head out of school, wanting to be only with myself and my thoughts. I find a bench near the football stadium, sit down, and scroll through more headlines, more news as it unfolds from Florida.

"There are numerous fatalities," Broward County Superintendent Robert Runcie said. "It is a horrific situation. It is a horrible day for us."

These teenagers were loving life one minute, laughing with friends and grumbling about tests, the everyday ordinary pace of a day. Now, they and everything they wanted, desired, dreamed of from life is gone... dead dead dead.

I open the favorites bar on my phone and press a button that dials the first number on the list.

"Dad? Did you hear about this shooting at a high school in Florida?"

"Oh, honey. Yes. It's so awful. I am so angry right now that this could have happened."

"I know. I hate this. I hate this so much."

"Can I do anything? Do you need anything?" he asks, his voice, tender and warm, soothing.

"No. But are you okay? Are you gonna backslide with this?"

"That's what I have my therapist for. I can talk to him if I need to. I'm not going to worry you with my problems. Let me know if we should make you an appointment, too. Maybe with me? We can talk all this out together."

"Dad, I'm glad you have that. But I need something different. I need to scream and be heard."

"Yes. You can change the world. It just takes one person. I believe that."

"Me, too. Love you."

"We'll get through this together. Promise?"

"Promise," I respond before ending the call.

I call up an Uber to take me home, still not wanting to talk to anyone right now. I pop in my earbuds and click over to my Jonas Brothers Spotify playlist as I wait for a blue Chevy Impala driven by Hudson to appear.

* * *

BRANDON

After the final bell rings, I grab my stuff and wait by the main entrance for Alli. After ten minutes of watching my breath freeze in midair, my hands shoved in my pockets to keep them toasty, students loudly rush by me, but she doesn't appear. I pull my right hand out of its cocoon to send Alli a *where r u* text. Minutes later, it's still unanswered.

Knowing I'm being ignored by my girlfriend on Valentine's Day weirds me out. *What the fuck?* I text Jimmy for a ride, and he thumbs that up, so I walk over to meet him at his car. Does this mean Alli is putting on the brakes? Are we moving too fast? Why is she blowing me off?

As I step into Jimmy's sight, I decide to get my mind off Alli dissing me. I look forward to hearing how he survived Valentine's Day and if Shelby embarrassed him with a singing Valentine.

I walk up as Jimmy is throwing his backpack in the trunk. He immediately announces: "Hey, did you hear? Someone lit up a school in Florida. I mean bad. The place is all shot up."

I don't respond. I open the car door, jump into the front passenger seat, and throw my backpack on the floor between my legs. I pull out my phone and go to the headlines.

> *Today, close to Marjory Stoneman Douglas High School's dismissal, students and staff heard what sounded like gunfire. The school immediately went on lockdown but is now dismissing students. We are receiving reports of possible multiple injuries. Law enforcement is on site.*

"Holy shit! This is bad. Really, really bad," I say flatly as I continue to scroll through first Twitter and then Apple News to read the shocking details.

> *So far, we have at least 14 victims. Victims have been and continue to be transported to Broward Health Medical Center and Broward Health North hospital.*

"Yeah. These wackos ruin it for everyone," says Jimmy as he pulls out of the parking spot. "It's the crazies with their guns who shouldn't be out on the street."

"No. They shouldn't. And on fucking Valentine's Day."

"And Ash Wednesday. This is a day to repent for your sins. Not be a sinner."

I continue reading about what went down as the news refreshes, my head buried in the headlines that leap up from my iPhone.

Shooter is now in custody. Scene is still active.

Is this why Alli blew me off? Because she's freaked out? I quickly text her and hit send.

Hey. R U OK?

Jimmy flips up the volume on the playlist cycling through his car speakers. Today, it's heavy on Two Door Cinema Club mixed with Run the Jewels, which weirdly works for me. I put away my phone and rest my head against the back of the seat, getting lost in the music.

Jimmy turns onto our street, both of us focusing on the beats vibrating from the dashboard. I'm in no rush to get home and learn more about this tragedy. In no mood for family dinner, family conversations today. I close my eyes as Post Malone's "Rockstar" washes over me.

After ditching my backpack in the mudroom, I grab a strawberry Pop-Tarts packet from the kitchen pantry. Standing at the kitchen sink, staring at the bare oak trees out the large glass window, I finish my sugar-glazed Pop-Tart in about six bites, washing it down with a glass of water from the tap. I flip on the small TV in the kitchen and stand motionless as I watch the horror unfolding on the television set.

Kids running. Cars and emergency vehicles with lights flashing backed up in a jumble on the street.

"It's devastating. I'm sick to my stomach," the Broward County sheriff, Scott Israel, explains.

As he talks, there are images of a cop in riot gear running with a gun, and then students walking outside with their hands straight in front of them or on top of their heads.

Seventeen people lost their lives. Twelve people within the building. Two people just outside the building. One person out on Pine Island Road, and two people lost their lives in the hospital. There are people still undergoing surgery.

Astor starts nudging me with her wet nose. "I know, I know," I say. Astor's all mine most days after school, since my parents usually don't get home from their jobs until after 6 p.m. My dad was working at Ford Motor Co. in Detroit thirty years ago when a headhunter offered him a management position at an aerospace manufacturing plant in Elk Grove Village, where he's been ever since. Mom works at a small recruiting company in Oak Brook, where she connects job-seeking ex-military officers with potential employers. It's a job she takes home with her, often entertaining us at dinner with success stories of the "matches" she's made.

I flick off the TV, grab the leash and my phone, and head out the door with the dog. Halfway down the block, my phone buzzes.

Alli sends me an emoji.

 TTYL.

I pull Astor over to a grassy patch to sniff.

OK.

I could say more. Like, "I hate this." Or, "Stay Strong." Something corny but sensitive. But I don't know what's up or down now, either. I have no answers. No comfort to give.

At dinner that night, Parkland is all we talk about.

My dad laments the irresponsible security guards, the slow response time from police.

I chime in abruptly, shutting it down before he can get out his next words. "There's gotta be a better way to keep crazy people from getting guns."

My mom and dad stare at each other over the supermarket-roasted chicken. "Dear. As you know, our nation was founded on certain rights," Mom begins, as she cuts into the chicken thigh on her plate. "To take those rights of self-defense, of gun ownership away from everyone because of the actions of one deranged person is not what our country stands for."

I listen as she spouts the Libertarian party line. I know it like the back of my hand. It makes sense to believe in personal responsibility. To believe in the right of self-defense. To reject violent behavior as abhorrent. Still. This carnage was caused by a teenager with an assault rifle. How many screwed-up teenagers do I pass in the hallway every day? A shit-ton of them probably.

"This killer is a kid who had gone to the school," I add forcefully.

"Yes. He did. He was very troubled. He needed help, and I am sorry to say he didn't get that in time, because adults did not do their jobs," my mom adds, to reassure me. To cement her point.

"He killed people he knows. Like at Columbine," I say, rattled by the images I've seen and the reality of what has happened at what was, just hours ago, an ordinary high school. "That just doesn't make sense to me."

"You have every right to feel that way, son," my dad says. "You're confused and upset. I get that. Of course, we can't just rely on the government to keep us safe."

"This is a dark, disturbing day," Mom adds. "But it's time for us all to be brave and fight back against evil, not to make the Bill of Rights our enemy."

I turn away from my mom's strong rhetoric and toward my dad, who has given me the best opening to end this topic of discussion tonight.

"It's the enemy I'm worried about," I explain. "It could be anyone at any time. And now I'm the one who has to walk into a high school tomorrow. Not you."

* * *

ALLI

I step in the front door to find my mom sitting on the sofa in the family room, hugging a pillow. Her eyes are glued to the television.

"Hi Mom," I say weakly.

"Hi, sweetheart. This is tough. Real tough."

I want to avoid. To not engage with this for a few moments. I walk over to where my brothers are building a Lego racecar on the carpet and kneel down next to them.

"Hey, Tommy. I love you," I say and give him a too-tight hug.

He grins widely at me, his tongue slightly purple from what I assume was a recently eaten popsicle or lollipop.

"Because it's Valentine's Day?" he asks.

"No, silly." I hug Sammy just as tightly. "Because I need you both to know that I love you every day."

He looks up from his pile of colorful plastic blocks. His bright eyes staring into mine melt my heart.

"Guess what, Alli?" Sammy teases. I smile for the first time in hours. He just has no idea how adorable he is. "We're going to a fish zoo tomorrow. Do you know what that is?"

I plop my butt down on the carpet, so happy to be in their innocent, beautiful world of fish zoos.

"*Hmm*... Is that like an aquarium maybe?"

"Yup," Sammy answers. "My teacher said an aquarium is just a big zoo for fish. Isn't that cool?"

"Super cool." I push myself up off the floor and join my mom on the sofa for a glimpse at what the big, bad world is up to now. It was just the medicine I needed, visiting the land of eight-year-olds. But now: reality.

We sit, numb, as the unfolding chaos plays out over and over. A line of students, each walking with hands touching the shoulders of the student in front of them. Then a tweet from Florida Senator Bill Nelson:

Our worst fears are being realized. It looks like it's a number of fatalities. Praying for all those students, families, and school members affected at Marjory Stoneman Douglas High School.

My dog, Murphy, pads over to sit on the floor at my feet. I lie on the sofa, stomach down, and rub the soft fur on his belly. His tail thumps with joy.

After more than an hour on the couch, staring at the TV and being bombarded with more horror, I realize I have to force myself to reengage with this fucked up world I live in. My mom walks back in and sits down next to me after driving my brothers to karate class.

"Mom, do you have cookie dough? Maybe that gluten-free break-and-bake stuff I like?" I need to do something comforting and mindless.

"No, sweetheart. Why don't you make dinner tonight? There's chicken tenders and the fixings for chicken parm in the fridge."

"*Ugh.* Do I have to? I'm spent and have homework to do."

Mom gives me a withering look.

I cave on the spot. I know my mind won't let me settle enough to study anyway, and the images from Parkland, from Marjory Stoneman Douglas, are making me increasingly anxious. I head to the kitchen on a mission to make an edible dinner for five and be distracted from my thoughts for a little while.

I ignore my phone all evening. I've answered the texts from Simone and Brandon with a few empty words that echo how I feel. Shell-shocked.

That night, I go to bed weighed down by the knowledge the bubble I have lived in and loved in and felt protected by here at home, in my neighborhood, inside my school, has burst. My dad's robbery showed me firsthand how the outside world is a scary place. But now, the whole of it is just as frightening.

I lie in bed and stare into the darkness. I can feel my mind begin to fade to black. The intensity of the day catches up with me, and I am beyond exhausted.

* * *

BRANDON

I wake up to a text from my sister Maura via our family group chat. She's been teaching English to high school students in Tokyo since last summer.

> *HFAC. Did you know Japan's never had a school shooting?*

That's Maura's go-to whenever she's pissed off, sad, or feeling angry: HFAC. Holy Flipping Animal Crackers. My sister Kelly and I have adopted it for when it suits our needs. There's a no-cursing rule in the Paulson house, so it's the one four-letter word our parents don't get uptight about us using.

Dad responds.

> *Japan is Buddhist. Also, they don't have Second Amendment.*

Maura texts:

> *17 dead. 17! What do you say to that?*

Shortly, there is a reply from Mom.

> *The school sheriff's deputy didn't do his job. The kid was mentally ill and on police radar but no follow up. This tragedy was avoidable.*

Then Kelly joins the conversation.

> *This time is different. The anger is real. You'll see.*

Maura voted for Obama and Hillary, and I'm pretty sure Kelly also went down the Hillary road. She didn't say. My sisters have made it clear they do not share our parents' Libertarian views, and we often avoid political talk because of it. But not today.

I read the texts, not sure where my voice fits. Or what I want to add. I want to thumbs-up Kelly's text. I agree with mom, too, though. That's the thing. I'm unnerved. I'm as mad as anyone. But I'm so HFAC confused.

As I prepare to reenter our upside-down world, I want nothing more than to be with Alli. I don't feel good about how she didn't want to talk or text with me. I'm sure she's shaken up.

Logistics make connecting for more than a minute between classes impossible for the time being. No car. No shared classes. I've already skipped study hall too many times. Then a light bulb goes off in my just-awakened brain: *I need to connect with Alli and figure out what is going on in her head.* We both need a mental health break this morning.

> *Do you want to grab breakfast?*

She texts me right back.

> *KK. We could both Uber to the Pancake House. Carbs are just what I need right now.*

I thumb-up her text, and by 8:30 a.m., we're sitting across from each other at a slightly wobbly table. I'm thinking pancakes. Bacon.

Alli's wearing a long-sleeve white top, the outline of her black bra evident beneath, and her blue Dolphin-logoed sweatpants. It's an unusual look for her, like she just rolled out of bed and grabbed the first thing from her closet.

"So. Rough day yesterday. How are you?"

She nods vigorously. "You know what I was thinking about when I woke up? About the empty desks. How hard it would be to sit in class the rest of the year with a desk that's empty, because a person was killed sitting in the same room as you."

"Alli. I mean *really*. Get that out of your mind. They aren't going to go right back to the same class. To the same rooms. I'm sure it's all going to be different. Sad, but different. Right?"

"I don't know. I guess so. I keep wishing all this was a bad dream. Did you talk about this with your parents last night?"

My emotions sit uncomfortably within me. I'm still sorting out so much in my mind about what went down in Parkland. What my family talked about, both last night at the dinner table and in our group texts.

I'm unsure how to explain my mindset to Alli when I am still working that out myself.

Just then, our waitress stops by the table with a pad and pen ready to go. We place our orders: Buckwheat pancakes and bacon for me. Coffee black. Oatmeal, wheat toast, and strawberries for Alli—and tea, of course.

"I'm really conflicted. I just can't process everything," I say once we're alone again. Alone together.

Alli nods.

"A school should not be a war zone. I'm so sad for the people who died. They were awesome. Every one of them. Awesome and doing great things. But then this guy. He's a fucked-up mess. He should have been stopped before. The signs were there."

"But he wasn't stopped," she says, staring straight into my eyes. "He had a gun he bought legally. Simone texted me. There's a rally on Friday. In memory. In honor. We're walking out of school third period. Will you come?"

I allow myself a minute to soak in Alli's genuine concern about how our fundamental beliefs don't line up. The problem is she doesn't realize what she's asking. She wants me to join this cheerleading squad she's part of for a team I have no desire to join.

"I need to know more. I need to understand the purpose. Is it to honor those who died? Is it about guns being evil?" I ask cautiously. "I just want to know what the walk-out is for. Don't judge. Just trust me to do what's best for me."

I peer down at my sweatshirt and pull out a small, navy-blue velvet pouch from the right pocket then place it gently on the table.

"I wanted to give you this yesterday, but it wasn't a typical day. So. Happy Valentine's Day." Sheepishly, I slide the pouch over to Alli.

She snatches it up quickly, clearly curious about the mystery inside. She places her finger inside to force the string open and then shakes the contents into her right palm.

A smile. A laugh. "I love it. Thank you!" she practically sings. The delight on her face is infectious. It's an emotion we haven't been allowed since yesterday afternoon, and it feels so liberating to share this pure moment of happiness together.

Alli unhooks the sterling silver clasp and drapes the silver chain around her neck, fastening it quickly. She glances down and strokes the small, sterling-silver dolphin as it lies against the base of her throat.

"Thank you. I may never take it off."

I am pleased with myself. My first foray into jewelry shopping for a girlfriend is a success. I had considered putting together a playlist for Alli, since Darcy was all over me after I made one for her last Valentine's Day on Spotify. But I am glad I decided to spend some dough. Alli is worth it. Besides, in her world, the Jonas Brothers represent the pinnacle of musical genius. I'm not sure what more I can offer.

Our waitress appears with a full, glass carafe and begins to pour, sloshing a little coffee into the saucer below my mug and even more onto the table. I grin faintly at Alli over her extended arm—my pretty, sensitive, but still tough-as-nails girlfriend.

* * *

ALLI

We sit quietly, watching our waitress's coffee-pouring skills, or lack of. When she walks away, ignoring the puddle she'd created, Brandon blots it up with his napkin then leaves the wet, brown ball at the edge of the table. When the waitress makes another trip to our table, she carefully sets down a small pot of hot water, lemon, and an Earl Grey tea bag in front of me and then whisks away the coffee-stained blob.

After she hands Brandon a crisp, white napkin from a stash in her apron, I check her nametag, written in blue Sharpie.

"Thanks, Sally," I say faintly.

"Your food will be right up," she responds briskly before stepping over to the table behind Brandon.

I launch into what's been eating at me since that day in Starbucks, when Brandon told me his parents are Libertarians. I need to understand what makes him tick.

"I want you to know. I'm totally against guns. And I think women have the right to make choices for their own body. And I hate Donald Trump."

"I'm pro-choice," Brandon declares, immediately. "And I'm not a fan of Trump's decision-making style. It's too reality TV for me." He pauses before addressing the one area still hanging out there.

"I mean, really, Alli, banning guns is not the answer. For me, it's much more involved than that."

I take a deep, calming breath, just as Coach Cam taught me to do on meet days, before I dive into the pool. To not let my emotions rule and potentially ruin a moment. And in this moment, I know I want to talk with Brandon, not fight with him.

"There's something I need to explain to you," I say, pushing aside the small plastic sugar holder and salt and pepper shakers from the middle of the table. I lay my palms flat on the table and meet his expectant gaze.

"Just this past June, my dad was alone with a customer in the pawnshop, and the guy pulled out a gun and pointed it at my dad's head and cocked it. He got away with some rings and made my dad clear out the cash register. They never caught him. My dad closed the store for two weeks, he was so freaked out about going back there."

I watch Brandon's expression change, as shock registers in his eyes. "Alli, that is so scary. I am so sorry that happened to him. That's a nightmare. I don't know what to say. This isn't something I'm used to talking about."

"Me, either. But now we need to. At least a little."

"Well, we've definitely done that. I get you, where you're coming from. I'm sorry about your dad. That's scary. And shitty."

I nod. I'm tired of talking about guns and death. Of being sad. There will be more time for that. Parkland just happened, and because of it, I feel both off balance and ready for battle.

"I need you to realize this is a big part of who I am now," I say. "My dad was a victim, but it's been hard on me, too."

Brandon moves his hand across the scratched linoleum table and grasps my fingers, holding them tightly. Not too hard. Not too soft. Just right. We sit quietly that way for a few drawn-out seconds until Sally reappears at our side.

We unlatch from each other as Sally places heaping plates in front of us. We dig in, turning the page to a new subject. For now, leaving questions unanswered.

* * *

BRANDON

After dinner, I head up to my bedroom and sit on the bed, leaning against the wall with a pillow behind me. I fire up my laptop to check in with Maura in Tokyo for our scheduled Facetime, catching her just as she's waking up.

"Hey, sis. How's your karaoke going?" I ask as she rubs her eyes and then runs her fingers through her sleep-tousled hair. Karaoke is her favorite topic of conversation these days. What she's singing. What her scores were at her last outing. How she has a dream to visit some karaoke room with a hot tub in it. I could go on.

"We rented a room with, like, twenty of us Friday night, and I got slammed for my version of 'Tiny Dancer.' Only a seventy-two. Oh well. I did better with 'Roxanne,' if you can believe that. An eighty"

"Ha! I can't picture you singing the Police. Or Elton John, actually. You've branched out since the early days of Madonna. I'm proud of you!"

"How are things there?" she asks. "I guess crazy, huh?"

"It's all so messed up. I have this girlfriend, Alli. I like her a lot. She swims for the Dolphins, and we're going to prom even."

"Oh, Brandon. Not swimcest. Tell me you didn't."

"Fuck off. That isn't funny," I snap, uncomfortable with her teasing. Swimcest is when swimmers on the same team date each other, which is easy to joke about, but I'd hoped my twenty-five-year-old sister would be past that level of annoying. "I don't swim for Cam anymore, anyway. I just quit."

"Oh. Well, congrats are in order then, I guess. Thanks for the update. You're right, that was in poor taste. Anyway, tell me about Alli."

"She has a scholarship to swim at Miami-Ohio, so she's super-serious about it. But with this Parkland shooting now, I think Alli's going to lose it. Her dad is dealing with serious mental shit after getting robbed at gunpoint last summer. So, she's a head case about guns already. She's super-emotional about her dad and how traumatized he is, and now, of course, this school shooting is freaking her out."

"That's really terrible. Where's your head at with all this?"

"I don't know. As much as I am pro-gun and really like hunting with dad, these school killings need to stop."

"It's all got to. So, how are Mom and Dad handling everything that is happening?"

"You know they won't change their tune even a little bit, so it's hard to talk to them about all this. And they don't know my girlfriend is involved now with these marches for stronger gun laws. So, that's going to be a fun conversation."

"I'm glad I'm six thousand miles away from that dustup."

"Why, you think it's going to be that bad? I mean, they liked that smelly vegan guy you dated the summer you waited tables at Maggie's. The guy with those huge gauge earrings and tattoos all over his arms."

"Says who? They never liked Luke. They basically tolerated him. And he did not smell, by the way. He had a unique scent because he used tea tree oil as deodorant. That's all."

"Oh. I always wondered what that stink was. They were super-friendly to him. Well, Alli is really great. And she smells normal."

"Then you have nothing to worry about. Just don't let them talk about politics. Or current events. Or anything in the news. Stick to safe topics."

"What's safe?" I ask.

"Yeah. That's a good question." Maura pauses to think for a second. "What's safe these days? Who even knows?"

* * *

ALLI

This much I believe. These lives lost must bring us together, not only in grief but in purpose. Doing nothing is not an option.

Lucky for me, Simone makes it easy to plug in. She's in Model UN and is almost as passionate about it as she is about swimming. She talked me into joining sophomore year, and while it was an eye-opening, world-expanding experience, it didn't click with me, so I stayed in my lane: the graphic arts club and the psychology club.

But I did get to know her Model UN partner, Justine, and had a front row seat to witness her passion about social justice. She's not just in tons of school clubs, like Amnesty International and Latina Dreamers, but even though she's a junior, she's president of the Empowerment Club. She's just the person I need to talk to. To learn from.

Justine. Can I help with the rally Friday?

Minutes later, I'm invited to join two Instagram accounts and one Twitter account.

Come to Room 414 today. The Empowerment Club meeting.

After school, I walk into the meeting. The room is full of unfamiliar faces, dozens of them. Justine grabs my arm and pulls me over to a chair next to hers in the front row.

"I'm glad you're here. We're going to make some noise tomorrow!"

After a few more minutes, the teacher, Ms. Arnold, closes the door. Everyone takes seats around the room, while a handful perch their butts on a long table pushed against the wall.

I do a double take when Ms. Arnold walks to the front of the room. She's dressed so much like my mom when she goes on sales calls— black top, straight-leg black pants, and black comfy flats. Ms. Arnold has added an unbuttoned dark-green cardigan, simple gold pendant earrings, and a long chain necklace that also could be straight out of my mom's closet. Her dark hair is tucked casually behind one ear, and she has an open, friendly expression.

"Thank you all for coming today," she says with a husky, slightly gravelly voice that sounds nothing like my mom's lively, cheerful tone. "I want to offer you this safe space to talk. To strategize about Friday and beyond. What we can do as a school not just to be heard but also listened to."

"What happens if we walk out of class tomorrow?" asks a lanky kid with blond hair. "I really need to get a parking space senior year, so I can't afford to get an unexcused absence."

Justine stands up and turns to face the back of the room, so all eyes are now on her. She may be only 5'2", but her cherry-red lipstick and black-framed eyeglasses give her a loftier stature. "Look," she tells us. "We're not going to have our mommies call us out of class. Resistance without consequence is not resistance."

"Yeah," the kid adds, "but I need that parking spot, Justine."

He is answered with pure silence. It's clear that every student here, except this nameless guy, knows, when Justine's got the floor, you shut up and listen.

"I'm happy to see a lot of new faces today," Ms. Arnold interrupts, switching gears. "Why don't some of you talk about what brought you. Why you are here."

Justine immediately turns to me. "This is my friend, Alli. It's her first meeting." She sits down and I really want to be mad that she's put me on the spot, except it's impossible to be mad at someone whose mission in life is to save the world.

"Welcome, Alli," Ms. Arnold says. "Why don't you tell us what brought you to our Empowerment Club meeting today?"

Planted at a desk with dozens of eyes trained on me, I spin my butt around in the chair. I decide to spill my guts about how I need to learn from this group of strangers.

"I have a confession to make. Before Parkland, before yesterday, I didn't know a thing about politics. Don't ask me to name our governor. I only know the name of one of our senators, Tammy Duckworth. But then Parkland happened, and now seventeen students and teachers have died. I don't want to be quiet or ignorant any longer. I have a scholarship to college, so I can't jeopardize that, but I do want to walk out. I do want to get involved."

"Me, too," a student says from the corner of the room.

"Me, also," another voice chimes in.

Soon, a chorus of "Me, too" reverberates around the room. What I said resonates. I'm happy to know I'm in the right place and with likeminded people who want to stand up for safe schools.

I also know there's a lot I didn't say about what I'm still grappling with. I'm dating a guy who believes what, exactly? And do his politics matter, when we're having fun, enjoying our final months of high school?

I need to understand what it means to be a Libertarian. I must understand why so many people believe gun ownership is an absolute right protected by the Second Amendment.

I want to form beliefs around guns that are grounded in something tangible and then be able to talk to Brandon and others about why my views are valid. That a high school senior shouldn't be able to buy any gun, much less an AR-15. I may not agree with Brandon, but I do respect that he is being true to himself. I get he has embraced his parents' values. Thank goodness he's so goddamn cute and sweet and makes me feel incredibly special whenever we're together. Isn't that all I need right now, anyway?

I tune back into the discussion going on around me. A girl in the back of the room is speaking.

"I'm not a political person, either," she says. I don't know her, but I already like the attitude on display. She wears a badass outfit—a black sweatshirt with SPIRITUAL GANGSTER in white-and-red splotchy block lettering, a flowy long red skirt, and black combat boots. "But suddenly, I feel vulnerable here. I feel scared. I just want to know. How can we feel safe at school?"

"That's something we all want. No matter what you believe about guns. We all want safe schools," says Ms. Arnold.

"Yes. So, this is what's gonna happen," says Justine, combing her fingers through her short, dark hair. "Send everyone you know an invite to our Instagram. The walkout is for tomorrow at 10 a.m. The walkout is just the first step. It's a statement."

"What comes next?" the lanky, blond "I need my parking spot" guy asks.

Justine casts her eyes around the room. We are all silent, wanting to know the answer to his question.

"Action, of course," she replies.

* * *

BRANDON

> *I have an English Lit test third period. But fingers crossed* 🤞 *still walking out. Will I see you there tomorrow?*

Alli texts me while I'm hanging at home with Astor at my feet, watching the Season 8 pool-party episode of *The Office* (again).

My fingers fly across my small keyboard.

> *Alli. I can't be around crazy, sign-waving students saying shit I don't believe. It's all too polarized now. Fill me in. OK?*

> *IDK. I think it sucks that you can't stand up for safe schools at least.*

> *That is not just what the march is about. It's about taking away guns. I'm not in same place you are.*

Obviously, Alli texts me back, trying to push me in a direction I don't want to go. I decide it's time to change the subject, even if it means texting about something boring.

> *How are your brothers? How's your training? Do you want to Facetime or hang out tonite? Something low key?"*

I try to lead us toward a lighter topic of conversation.

I check my phone. And again, after dinner. As the hours roll by, I check it again, again, again. But nothing. Nada from Alli.

By midnight I realize I'm being ghosted by my girlfriend. *Great. Just great.* So much for talking it through.

* * *

ALLI

I stare at the round, white clock face at the front of the classroom. Its hands read 9:57.

"So," I say, turning to Topher, who sits next to me in Ms. Elstrom's English lit class. "When the clock strikes ten, is this going to happen?"

Topher immediately perks up. "Damn straight it is."

The next thing I know, a voice blares into our classroom from an intercom near the door. Claudia Vasquez, our school's beloved activities director who's been here since forever, announces, "If you are going to the school walkout, leave now, and exit through the main entrance."

"Should we bring our backpacks?" Topher asks Ms. Elstrom.

"No. No backpacks. Leave them," she answers briskly. "I'll be here."

All but four of the students in class stand up. I join the line filing out the door and launch my body into the throng of students quietly marching down the hallway to leave the school.

Gabi appears beside me with a smallish piece of cardboard under her left arm that reads in blue bold letters *NOT ONE MORE*. I think back to how she was the first person I saw at that terrible moment when I learned about the madman with a gun at a high school in Florida. She pulls me closer and leans over to whisper in my ear.

"This doesn't feel like a protest. Like a statement. The teachers and school are all, like, 'March and shout about guns and then come back to class ASAP.'"

I nod sadly. But this is what we have in front of us now, today. So, I hope we can make the best of it. "Yes, I agree. But I think the larger point is our saying that things need to change, combined with thousands of other schools saying the same thing. That means something bigger, right?"

Gabi starts to fidget with her nails. "Yeah," she says, studying the cuticle she's just destroyed. "I guess." The crowd around us swells as we walk through the open front doors and head outside. Then, she grabs at the sign with her right hand and disappears into the mob of bodies milling around somewhat aimlessly.

Suddenly, Justine appears at the top of the steps outside the main entrance. She's holding a megaphone and speaks forcefully into it. Although I find a spot halfway into this huge mass of students, I cannot hear a word she says.

My eyes sweep the crowd. Tyler is planted next to two police officers, who stand at the fringes, alert. He has a white earbud in one ear, and my blood starts to boil at his level of asshole-ness. Tyler was my least favorite person on our club swim team. The day I heard he was switching over to play water polo in high school, I dragged Simone out to split an ice cream sundae with me after practice. We celebrated so hard, I almost put myself in a sugar coma.

I see a few red MAGA hats, which confuses me. I read a sign: *Guns Make Us Safer. Change My Mind.* That further confuses me.

Most of my fellow students are standing at attention and respectfully watching the two students who follow Justine on stage. Thankfully, now the speakers are using a microphone, but I assume the crowd around me still cannot hear a word, since I sure can't. Phones are out in force to capture this moment to share with friends, moms, Instagram, Snapchat, or just for posterity.

"Well, this sucks," I say to a guy in front of me. I remember seeing him at the Empowerment Club meeting, but I never learned his name.

He nods. "The sound system is just bad," he says. "I know they tested it, so not sure what happened."

Suddenly, the crowd erupts into a chant. "*Enough Is Enough*" and then another, "*No More Guns.*"

The student speakers who stand on either side of Justine raise their right arms to the sky over and over again as, together, we chant loudly. Our voices carry across the parking lot and more signs are held high. *Protect Children, Not Guns,* one reads. A tall, gangly girl holds a sign that breaks my heart into a million pieces: *Am I next?* A dad stands slightly on the edge of the crowd, alongside a handful of random adults who I assume are other students' parents. His sign freaks me out the most:

> *I shouldn't have to worry if a CORONER is going to pick my daughter up from school instead of ME.*

These signs make me want to lose it right there and then. And just like that, the seventeen minutes that the march was scheduled to take place—one minute for each of the students and teachers killed in Parkland—ends in a whimper. Students file back to class. The solemn vigil gives way to what feels like normal, boisterous, everyday energy.

Sad and angry thoughts overwhelm me as I trudge up the stairs for the waning minutes of Ms. Elstrom's class.

Brandon wasn't there. He missed it all. He should have showed he cared enough to stand by my side and honor seventeen brave souls. This march felt hard and sad and brutal. He should have been there, even if he wanted to hang around with the MAGA-hat guys. Instead, he took the easy way out.

* * *

BRANDON

After school, I walk into my quiet house feeling empty. Being ghosted by Alli sucks. I wish she would just understand how twisted this day was for me. How I could not stand next to signs that say all guns are evil or whatever shit was going down at the march.

Astor scampers up to my leg and starts to nudge me, begging for her walk. I want to ignore her eagerness, but I know she's had a tough day, too, stuck inside all by her doggie self. So, I grab the leash, and we start our loop around the block.

As we walk, Astor pees on a few trees, sniffs the grass, and trots by my side, while I think about how I cannot recall a time growing up when my parents weren't engaging with politics and world history. Magazines like *Reason* sat on our coffee table next to *National*

Geographics. Since podcasts have become a thing, my mom and dad fill our family group texts with recommendations, usually hour-long broadcasts by Ben Shapiro or *This American Life,* which they'd listened to on their car rides to and from work and wanted to share with us.

Every summer since I was thirteen, my dad and I would take part in an Appalachia Service Project together. We traveled to a small town in Tennessee and met up with some of Dad's Marine buddies and their teenage sons. Over a hot, hectic forty-eight hours, we'd put in full days helping seniors stay in their homes by installing wheelchair ramps, widening doors, and adding grab bars. At night, we would sit around a campfire or at a long dinner table in a diner, where the dads' talk would inevitably turn to the places the families had rolled through in their RVs on their way to the Project that year; the various tornadoes, rainstorm floods, or hurricanes each of them had survived over the past year; plus boring updates about pets and family members back home, and some lighthearted jabs about one another's beloved pro football teams. Then came angry talk about the war started by Bush, Junior that seemed never to end and had devolved into a hellhole for the soldiers and the US of A.

As the nights went on, I heard it all. "Obamacare is socialism creeping into our lives." "Hillary should be sent to jail, not the White House." Over and over again, my dad and his friends would complain about the liberal wackos who blamed the NRA for gun violence, when they knew the NRA just helped protect their rights. Take away those rights, they said, and you would be denying people their liberty, their privacy, and their freedom.

It makes sense to me.

Alli and I are looking outward at different realities. Still, that doesn't mean we should stop trying. I'm not giving up on us that easily.

Hey, I heard the march was a bit unorganized but also intense.

I text her. And then I wait.

* * *

ALLI

"Mom, I need your advice," I announce, as I slide down next to her on the gray sofa in our formal living room, the room reserved for adults.

"Okay, shoot," she says, putting her stack of mail down on the glass coffee table.

"Well, that's the problem, actually. Shooting. I went to the March for Our Lives vigil today. It was intense and scary and sad. Everyone was chanting, 'No More Guns,' and some people had signs, so I guess we're making a statement. I hope so."

"I get that. It's scary. I don't envy your generation. Ours is not getting the message that there have to be stronger gun laws. It's important to keep saying it, though."

"Well, that's the thing. I am mad that Brandon didn't go. He feels like the march had an agenda that's skewed against what he believes in. So, he wouldn't stand in solidarity with us."

"Seriously? Did you tell him about your dad and the robbery?"

I nod and curl myself into my mom's arms. "But, Mom, in a way, he was right. He said he thought the march would be about guns and not about the victims. I guess it was about both. It was about guns and the NRA and how they both suck. How can it not be?"

"So, are you broken up then?"

"Not sure. Should I break up with him because of this? I really, really, really like him, Mom. But then, this is fucking with my mind."

"Honey, watch your language. I think looking at situations from different vantage points is okay, if you're happy together. That's part of growing up—learning to discuss your values with people you care about and respect those differences." She pauses, and I snuggle deeper into her embrace.

"Did I ever tell you," she continues, "how my own dad knew I wanted Hillary Clinton to win, and on election day he called to tell me he'd voted Libertarian, because he didn't like Trump or Hillary? I told him that was a cop-out, and he just said I shouldn't make an issue of it, because Illinois would go for Hillary anyway. That my vote would count but his wouldn't matter. I wanted to be upset with him, but how could I? He's my dad."

"That's basically what Simone says. To just let this stuff roll off."

Mom nods, and we sit silently on the sofa, staring into space with our thoughts, as she strokes my hair.

"Shit!" Mom yells, jumping up abruptly.

I lose my anchor, and so I stand up alongside her after she's put me off balance.

"I have to get the boys at karate. I lost track of time." She rushes into the kitchen to grab the car keys. "Sorry, hon. I'm not a good mom, telling you not to curse, and then I do just that. But I have to pick up your brothers," she says as I follow behind her.

"Go, Mom. I'm fine. You helped. A lot."

"I hope so. That's my number-one job. To help you figure out this messy world."

And then she is gone, out the door.

After she backs the minivan down the driveway and out of sight, I grab my phone and text Brandon.

What are you doing? Wanna hang out?

* * *

BRANDON

My eyes light up at the text that comes through my phone. I start to type quickly but then let my finger linger in the air for a few seconds before sliding it over to my favorites and clicking on her number.

Alli picks right up. "Hey."

"Hey. I'd love to hang, but not tonight. I'm all sweaty and exhausted. Guess what I just did?"

"Seriously, Brandon? How would I know?"

"I ran. Four miles."

"I thought you hated running."

"Why did you think that?"

"Because I hate running and Simone hates it, and it seems like every swimmer I know hates it. That's why."

"Well, that's true. But playing Ultimate means I have to stay on top of my game. Since I don't happen to have an indoor pool in my house, what else can I do? Pizza and burgers are my two favorite food groups, so I have to keep kicking my butt. Four miles is my limit. Want to run with me one day?"

"No, thanks. I'd try Ultimate, though."

"Sorry. Guys only."

"That's okay. I don't have the time anyway. Did you realize when you quit swimming that you'd be giving up your workouts?"

"So worth it, though. So worth it. Anyway, how are you?"

"I'm okay. Guess what I just did?"

"Seriously, Alli? How would I know?"

"I texted you. Do you know why?"

"Because you missed my brilliant wit?" I say hopefully.

"Exactly."

"I miss you, too. Change of plans. I'll come over later. Does that work?"

The phone goes silent. I hold the phone away from my ear and eye it warily, to see if we got disconnected, but the seconds keep ticking by. I return the phone to my ear.

"Alli?"

Nothing. I start to cycle through our conversation and what I may have said to piss her off. We were so close to being a normal couple again. *Where did things go wrong?* Then I hear her voice on the line.

"I just texted with my mom. If you can get here in forty-five minutes, you can join us for family dinner. We're having pizza and salad, and you just ran four miles, so you earned it. My stepdad refs basketball games at the Y on Friday nights, so we're eating kinda early because of my brothers."

I exhale my worries at the sound of her voice. "Sounds awesome. I'll bail on the spinach quiche my mom is making. See you soon." My heart dies a little as I finish that sentence. My mom knows I love her dinners of spinach quiche with sausage and peppers, which is most likely why she is making it tonight. She's not going to be happy with the disappearing act I'm about to pull.

"Are you going to shower first, though?" Alli asks hesitantly.

"To eat with *your* family? Of course. I'm not a caveman."

"Perfect," Alli answers as we both hang up and I head downstairs, knowing I am now the bad son about to ruin his mom's evening.

* * *

ALLI

Why did I think this was a good idea? I look over at my two brothers shoving pizza into their mouths like they haven't eaten in a week. As they chew, with tomato-tinged lips, they smile at Brandon—a strange, six-foot-tall addition to our dinner table.

"Brandon, I hear you just stopped swimming with the Dolphins. How's that going?" my mom asks as she wipes her hands on a white paper napkin.

"It's definitely an adjustment. But I was burned out, so it was time. I've been running 'cuz I need to keep myself in shape. So far, so good," he answers, dropping his hands to his sides.

"I do karate," says Tommy. "I'm a white belt with two stripes," he adds proudly.

Sammy nods enthusiastically. "I do karate, too. Do you want to come to our belt test? It's when we get more stripes."

"Me?" Brandon points to himself as he grins at my brothers. "Sure... When is it?"

Two little faces look to my mom for the scoop.

"Oh, the belt test. It's Sunday, boys. At 9 a.m. Don't you think you should invite your sister to go, too, though?" Mom asks with a sly smirk.

"Sure, she can come," answers Tommy before munching on his pizza crust.

"I feel so welcome," I say warmly. My brothers don't realize how much I love that they want Brandon, whom they just met, more than their beloved sister at their super-boring but so, so cute belt test.

"Wow, I'd love to see your belt test," Brandon says. "But I'm going to Wisconsin this weekend with my dad."

"That sounds fun. What are you doing there?" my mom asks innocently.

"Oh, he's taking me trapping. It's a father-son trip with some of his Marine buddies."

"So, you can't go?" Tommy asks.

"Next time, okay?"

"Yes, he'll try to be there next time," I say. "You're stuck with just me."

"Your dad is a Marine? *Wow!*" Sammy says, his face lit up, totally ignoring my yes RSVP.

"That's cool!" echoes Tommy, always needing to make sure he adds his voice to his brother's.

"What's cool about it to you?" I ask, interested in hearing the next words to fall from their little mouths.

"Alli, that's enough," my mom interjects, adding, "You know better."

"Excuse me." I realize I sound defensive. I stand up and start to pile the empty plates into the sink. "I just wanted to learn more. I am in AP Psychology, you know. It's what we do."

"Not with your brothers you don't. They don't need any psychoanalysis from their sister."

"*Fine!* I have to show Brandon something in my backpack, Mom. Okay?"

"Thanks for dinner, Mrs. Nixen," Brandon says as he stands up and pushes in his chair.

"Of course. You're welcome anytime," Mom adds, forever the diplomat.

Brandon and I tramp up the stairs to my room, and Brandon shuts the door behind us. *Good move.* He sits on my bed, and I twirl around on my desk chair until I face him.

"Alli, what's up with you? You totally embarrassed me in front of your family," he says with a slight frown.

"I just wanted to hear what they thought was so intriguing, you know."

"No, not really."

I walk over to where he's sitting on my bed and plop down so our bodies are touching. "Okay, okay, I get it. Don't be mad at me—I didn't mean anything by it. I just was interested in what eight-year-old minds think is cool. What are you trapping, anyway?"

"Beavers. But I don't want to feel judged by you or your family."

"Beavers? Really? They sound cute."

He starts to stand up. "I'm leaving. I didn't come here for this," he says sharply.

"You're right. No more judgment, I promise." I tug at the hem of his shirt and he turns toward me.

He leans slightly in and kisses me full on. I know I'm lucky he can shake off the attitude I just put on full display.

"Maybe ditch the amateur psychology," he suggests, sitting back down on my bed.

I so like this guy! Tonight, he charmed my mom and my cute brothers, and he's won me over completely. I move closer and we're kissing, probing, wanting.

"Alli!" my mom yells up the stairs. "Can you finish the dishes and walk Murphy?"

I quickly untangle myself from his arms. "*Okay, in a few!*" I yell back. "The closed bedroom door is obviously more than she wants to handle right now," I explain to Brandon.

He shrugs. "I gotta go, anyway. I told my mom I'd be home early because it's Kelly's twenty-first birthday, and we're going to Facetime her at eight. My mom even bought a birthday cake. And then I'm going over to Jimmy's later to hang."

"That's fun," I say, secretly frustrated my Friday night is turning into such a dud.

"Is there really something in your backpack you want to show me?"

"What do you think?" I answer, flashing a coy smile.

We only have a few more minutes tonight to hang out together. So, we make the best of it.

* * *

MARCH 2

BRANDON

Since there's no school on Monday, turning a three-day weekend into a four-day weekend turns out to be too much of a temptation to resist for many of my senior classmates. Without fail, whatever class I walk into, half the chairs are empty.

"You know who's here today, don't you?" Evan says, smirking as he slides in behind me after I open the door to our English Literature class. "It's the athletes who can't miss their games, plus anyone who hasn't chosen a school yet."

Way to rub it in, Evan. "I'm here because I want to be," I reply. I paste on a fake grin, knowing Evan has no idea I'm being sarcastic. I've known Evan since middle school. He's a total computer geek with zero social graces, and he's already in at, like, four colleges. It's obvious he doesn't share my uneasiness that we aren't part of today's senior ditch day.

Our English teacher, Mr. Goldman, asks those of us who showed up to pull our chairs into a circle. He passes out a stack of graphic novels and asks us each to take one. I pull *Pride of Baghdad* from the pile and start to leaf through it.

"Today, we are going to spend our class time becoming familiar with different genres of graphic novels," he tells us, adding, "Your assignment, due next week, will be to write a graphic short story."

"We have to draw it, too?" asks Maya, tentatively.

"Yes. That's what makes it a graphic short story." Mr. Goldman's matter-of-fact delivery elicits laughter from some parts of the room.

I hope he likes stick figures, because that's my highest level of artistic talent.

I stare down at the images, which leap out from the page: four lions, the war, and their escape from the Baghdad Zoo.

I'm sitting next to Chris, who is wearing a Hawks baseball shirt— I think he's a pitcher. "Man," I say to him, "this is the most intense comic book I've ever seen."

"I'll take a graphic novel over a book with a gazillion words any day," he replies, waving the book cover for *El Deafo* in my face.

"Good point." I nod with a new appreciation for the story in my hands.

As the minutes tick by, my classmates and I swap graphic novels around the circle and point out favorite imagery to students sitting nearby. Mr. Goldman gives us a free pass, sitting at his desk immersed in a stack of papers, and I'll take it. I exchange my book with a girl sitting to my right, Bethany.

"*Ugh*, chick lit," I say out loud. Its cover, *SLAM!*, is pink, green, and yellow, with a girl wearing a helmet. Bethany scowls at me and turns away. "Sorry," I add, not quite sure why I'm apologizing. I mean, a book on girls' roller derby is not something I'm into reading, even if it is in comic book form.

My phone vibrates, and I yank it out, happy for the distraction. It's a text from my dad, reminding me he's picking me up for a dentist appointment after school, which is a downer, so I switch over to check the latest in my inbox.

Seconds after pulling up my email, I can't help but scream, "*YES!*" at the top of my lungs.

Mr. Goldman looks my way with a frown. "Mr. Paulson," he says, scolding.

"I'm sorry, Mr. Goldman. But I'm in at Wisconsin. I just got the email!"

"Ah. Well, congratulations, Brandon. In that case, holler away."

A few of my classmates clap, and Evan walks over to pat me on the back awkwardly.

"Can I be excused to tell my parents?" I ask.

He nods, and I shoot out into the hallway in a flash. My first thought is that I want to tell Alli the good news. But I realize there is a list I must cycle through first, including my parents and my fellow-Badger sister. Plus, I have to wait to WhatsApp my sister Maura after dinner. Our days are still their nights, so, right now, she's fast asleep.

* * *

ALLI

Our basement is a wonderland of boy toys: Nerf guns, trains, trucks, and Legos mingle in jumbled piles. I clear it all out of the way so Brandon and I can shoot some pool.

The pool table is Ray's. The story I've heard my mom tell people a hundred times is that it was moved from the dining room of his bachelor apartment. Over the years, he's done his best to teach both me and my mom his tricks, but she is embarrassingly horrible at pool. She has a knack for knocking in the eight ball and sinking the cue ball, sometimes in the same stroke. I'm the only family member Ray can compete against without his eyes glazing over. Clearing a table is no big deal for me.

"Shit, Alli, you didn't tell me you're badass at this," Brandon remarks, leaning against his cue stick and marveling at how I just sunk three striped balls in succession.

"I love shooting pool. It's the one thing Ray and I connect over. He's a great teacher."

"Can he give me some lessons? Seriously. I'd love be known as the Wisconsin pool shark—and not the wet kind."

"*Ha*! That's a good one. I'm sure he would. Do you want me to ask him to come down now? I think he's home."

"Nope." Brandon rushes his answer as I'm talking. "I just want us to hang. I like this. But I'll take some pointers from you." He studies the table. "So?" The cue ball is sitting at the edge of the green felt, an inch from the wood frame.

"Those shots are hard. I would just whip it to sink six."

He tries to follow my advice. The cue ball tickles the green solid, and it rolls slowly, slowly, slowly over to the left pocket. Then stops a hair short. He strides over and blows on the ball to topple it in, but it stays teasingly close to the edge of the pocket.

I keep my smile bottled up, as I don't want Brandon to see me acting smug. I feel his eyes watching me as I zone in on the striped balls to find my next move. I know I can be so serious about things that are important to me. Right now, top of that list is beating Brandon at pool.

"So, now that you are in at Wisconsin, do you think you'll do the ROTC program there, like your parents?" I ask casually as I chalk the cue stick.

"Can't we just shoot pool? Why do we have to talk too?" Brandon sounds annoyed, clearly trying to deflect my comment.

"You don't want to talk about it? Really?"

"No. I don't, Alli. I don't want us to fight again."

"So, now you think I won't be supportive of you being in ROTC? That's crazy. I think it's very cool, actually."

"You do? I just don't know where the boundaries lie with us sometimes. That dinner conversation with your family last week was exhausting. So yes, I'm taking the elective course freshman year. It's a great leadership program. And it's gonna help me decide if I'm Army or even maybe Marine material. I'm definitely interested."

"I know. I invited you over for pizza, not the first degree. Sorry. I don't really know people who've been in the military except your parents, to be honest. Anyway. Sergeant Paulson. That sounds important."

"I would be a private," he says. "But thanks for the promotion."

"Anytime. Happy to be of service." I walk over behind the cue ball. Brandon has conveniently left it exposed, so I have a clear shot in two directions. Studying the configuration in front of me, I purse my lips to figure out which striped ball of the three left on the table I want to strategically put away.

* * *

BRANDON

Jimmy's obsession with Ultimate Frisbee is legendary. He's not only skilled and has competed in tournaments on both coasts, but when he wakes up, his first move is to check the weather, hoping it's gonna cooperate, so he can get a game going. And since Ultimate needs only one thing, a Frisbee, I often hang out in his world of pickup Ultimate. Turns out, swimming is great training for moving a Frisbee down the field, since I can run forever and my lungs don't give out. Put Jimmy and me on the same team, and we're basically unstoppable.

Today is no exception. It's an almost fifty-degree March day, so Jimmy immediately organized a huge game at Vanguard Park. His Ultimate GroupMe brought out a crowd of juniors and seniors. We had a full field, with seven players on each side and two alternates. It took almost ninety minutes for us to lock it up. In the end, we won 15-12.

Jimmy is one of the few guys I will really miss when I go to college in the fall.

"Too bad you couldn't hang with us yesterday. We had a blast in Chicago," he tells me as we collapse onto the grass, our chests heaving, after the last power play down the line cinched our win.

"Well, I had a good day, too. I'm a Badger for life now."

He rolls up from the grass and props his elbows over his knees. "I knew you'd get in. As of September, we have to become enemies. Isn't *frenemies* a word? And we'll hate on each other when Illini plays you guys."

"Yes," I exclaim. "Frenemies we will be!"

"So, my sister was in the school's Shakespeare play this weekend," Jimmy says as we walk up to my car. "I had to go. I thought it was going to be torture, but it wasn't half bad. *Midsummer's Night Dream.* Wanna know my favorite part?"

"The end?" I ask.

"No, seriously. You'll love this. Patrick and Bryant get in this sword fight, and Patrick's sword just breaks. Like the tip just falls right off. Seriously. Bryant is so shocked, he steps back, bumps into a tree, and the tree falls down. It was epic."

"That's sad, Jimmy. You like the most twisted shit." I flip the key fob to unlock my car door. Jimmy's brother is in town, so, at least for today, he's riding shotgun. We both climb into the car, and the doors shut in unison.

"I have five bucks with me. Is that enough for two Slurpees?" I ask.

"Sure." Jimmy settles himself into the passenger seat. "As long as you're not getting the huge cup that's as big as your arm."

"I may go for the big one. We need to celebrate me getting into Wisconsin!"

* * *

ALLI

"Mom, are you coming to my swim club award night next Wednesday?" I ask as I'm emptying the dishwasher and she's putting away two bags of groceries in the kitchen. "It starts at 6 p.m. at the high school."

"Oh, that's right. It's the twenty-first," Mom says. Her eyes narrow and her forehead creases, which I know means she's busy cycling through her mental to-do list. "Yes, I would like to be there. Let me make sure Ray can be home with the boys."

"Dad's coming too, FYI."

"Honey, that's fine. Just fine. Steven and I are friends. Well, we're friendly."

"I know. It's just you haven't seen him in a while. I wanted to give you a heads-up."

"I appreciate that, I do," Mom says. "What can I bring?"

"Oh, yeah. Like, chips and salsa maybe?" I answer as I snap the dishwasher door shut. "I'll ask my swim teammate, Kaitlyn, since her parents are in charge of organizing the potluck."

* * *

BRANDON

Once you've sent in the deposit to your first-choice college, high school gets especially painful. I sit down at my computer, and while I should be knocking out my graphic novel short story, I pull up Google Maps and type something completely unrelated to my assignment into the search bar.

I learn there are 430 miles between University of Wisconsin in Madison and Miami University in Oxford, Ohio. I mess around with the travel icons to figure out that the distance can be driven in six hours, thirty minutes. Which is a long-ass time to be in a car.

Or I could fly in three hours from Madison's airport to Cincinnati, Ohio's, for $300. Which is both complicated and expensive.

I then pull up the Miami-Ohio women's swim team site, to read what teams they compete against in their division. I was not expecting to see Wisconsin on the list, and that is what happened.

Maybe I'm getting ahead of myself by making these calculations.

I need to get a grip, because I'm really falling for this girl. In less than six months, we'll be hundreds of miles away from each other. I want to enjoy this time we have and not fight over stupid politics.

Part of me wants to go to college unattached. To join a frat, hook up tons, and never look back. But another part of me cannot picture my life without Alli in it.

Seeing the distance between our universities further hardens my resolve to not get too serious. To not tell Alli I love her.

It's just so frustrating when my heart and my head are not on the same page. I need them to be because, although I'm falling hard for Alli, when this summer is over—I have to be real—so are we.

* * *

ALLI

I'm sitting at the white fake-wood desk in my room, facing my bulletin board. The summer before I started high school, I nailed this huge corkboard into the white wall and used thumbtacks to fill every inch with photos. Photos of me when I was eight, riding a horse and wearing a cowboy hat as big as I was. Photos of me with Simone at one of our many swim meets, or with my dad at a Cubs game. Me toasting marshmallows with my brothers on a beach vacation in Michigan when I was twelve. Photos that usually make me smile inside and out. Except now, I'm not in a smiling mood. The history paper I'm attacking, my last high school paper ever, is giving me a headache. *Write about a federal or state legislative law that you believe should be reversed or changed and why.*

I'm heavy into edits on this final paper when a small box pops up in the corner of my computer with a message from Simone. I am so happy for the excuse to click out of my paper. I open my phone to check in with the picture she's texted me.

It is a full-length photo of Simone looking so incredibly pretty in a long, navy-blue dress with a band of sparkles encircling her waist and thin spaghetti straps.

Love, I message her.

My prom dress. For now.

It's your color IMO.

I know! Right?

I wonder if this is *THE DRESS.* A lot of girls buy multiple dresses before deciding which one hits all the Musts:
  * I must look incredible.
  * I must not trip and fall and look stupid because the dress is too long.
  * I must be able to dance in it at least a little bit.
And the most important must:
  * I must have a dress that nobody else at my high school has.

That's why Adrienne, our school's most serious fashionista, started a Facebook page for us girls, where we could all post photos of our prom dresses. I haven't checked it out yet, so I click over to it now.

To be honest, I had my eyes on an eerily-similar sapphire-blue dress with spaghetti straps from Bloomingdale's online. It's $150 with twenty-percent off, and I was going to show it to Mom this weekend. Now that Simone has snagged hers, though, I will have to be open to other colors. But no pink; no black.

* * *

BRANDON

I skip study hall to hang outside with Alli during her lunch. We sit across from each other at a table next to the football stadium, and I help her dig into a small bag of veggie chips. I have news to share with her.

"My sister's good friend has a brother, Charlie, who's going to Wisconsin," I begin, "we just texted. And I think I have a roommate. He seems really chill. Totally not a guy I would become friends with normally, but I think he'll be a solid roomie."

"What's wrong with him? I mean, how can you choose a roommate you wouldn't want as a friend."

"Oh, it's not like that. I just don't see us hanging out. He plays drums in a jazz group and is going to try out for the marching band, so odds are he won't be a frat-bro roommate who's gonna barf on our carpet, which Kelly says is the key."

"Actually, that does sound pretty good. So, it's a done deal?"

"We didn't confirm it. I hope I didn't sound like that frat-drunk roommate to avoid, because I do want to lock it in. I'll let you know."

"Why? What'd you say?"

"Well, I did tell him I want to be a Sigma Chi. Hey, I never asked you. Do you have your roommate figured out?"

"I'm gonna live with another swimmer, because we both will be on the same crazy early training schedule that not many roommates would want to put up with. I don't know who yet, but I think we'll become good friends, as we'll go through hell week training together and need someone to cry to."

"Oh man, that sounds bad. What's hell week at Miami-Ohio supposed to be like?"

"Do you remember Samantha? She was on our club team a few years ahead of us? She's swimming at Miami-Ohio and already warned me the first two weeks of practice will be pure misery. There's a daily hard-ladder swim and an IM set at a killer race pace. Doesn't that sound awful?"

"I don't remember her but, Alli, that sounds miserable. Are you sure you're up for that?"

"Well, there's only one way to find out. Of course, my dad wants me training hardcore here, so the workouts don't kick my ass too hard. But I don't think it's possible to prepare for something so intense. I just have to do what I can do and hope for the best."

"Well, I'll be going through hell week, too... *Rushing!*"

She starts to laugh. "I hear they don't let you sleep and force you to chug beer nonstop."

"I doubt I'll be drinking beer nonstop. But yeah, I will be drinking a shit-ton of it. We'll have to compare notes," I add.

"Yes, and I think you will win! Your hell week will be worse than mine."

* * *

MARCH 17

ALLI

I managed to secure my stepdad's car today, since he's working from home, and I've earned a few brownie points by volunteering to watch my brothers while Mom and Ray go out to dinner tonight. I haul my swim bag into the back seat after swim practice and jump in the driver's seat with my phone in hand. A backlog of messages has piled up since I walked into the locker room three hours ago. After scrolling through dozens of texts and GroupMe's, I text Philip that I'm game for hanging out tonight and I'm bringing Brandon and cookies.

I know it's very 1950's housewife of me to be known as the girl who shows up to a party with cookies on a covered paper plate. But break-and-bake cookies are just so easy and so damn delicious. And they make everybody happy. Me included.

Want to go to Philip's house tonight? He's having some people over, and I don't have practice tomorrow.

Brandon texts back within seconds.

Sure. I love Philip's man cave.

The summer before ninth grade, Philip's parents told him that he and his younger brother and sister could turn the walk-up attic into their own hangout space. Every Christmas since, his wish list has focused on stocking this space. It has a huge TV, a foosball table, and a mini-fridge. There's a grungy, once-white sofa encircled by massive, red, square pillows that are really comfy to sit on. I always head straight for the pillows, as that sofa is just tinted too gray for my taste.

I can drive. I have a car tonight. It may be nine. I'm gonna hang with my brothers while my mom and Ray go out. I'll text you to confirm, but they never stay out late.

OK. 9 is good.

After my mom and stepdad leave for the restaurant, I sit on the family room couch with my brothers in their cozy pajamas. Sammy's are covered in baseballs, while Tommy's long PJs are striped in blue and gray. I open a well-worn hardcover copy of *Charlotte's Web*, and they snuggle close on either side of me. They love Wilbur the Pig's story, and I love reading it to them.

After we've relished Charlotte's "some pig" handiwork, I lead the boys into the kitchen and grab two packages of refrigerated chocolate chip cookie dough from the fridge.

"Sammy, why don't you grab two baking sheets," I say, pointing at the cupboard to the right of the oven. He clangs around the dark expanse before pulling out the two pans and dropping them on the white Formica countertop. They clatter noisily.

I separate out the tiny squares with a dull knife and then give Tommy the aerosol spray can of olive oil. Within seconds, he completely coats one large baking pan but that doesn't stop the spraying.

"Whoa, there! That's enough," I warn, as I wrestle the can away from his little fingers.

"My turn," Sammy pipes up, reaching for the can and pulling it right out of my grasp. He triple-greases the second cookie sheet until I have to grab the canister from his fast-moving hands, too.

The boys then randomly plop the squares down on the oily pans, sliding them around like cars, so they crash into each other again and again.

"Okay, enough bumper cars," I say, rescuing the cookie sheets to realign the cookie squares and slide them into the hot oven. I'm feeling a little guilty about this being not the most hygienic way to bake for my friends.

* * *

BRANDON

"I'm going out with Alli tonight. She's picking me up around nine," I announce, standing in front of the speckled granite kitchen island, eyeing my dinner choices. Salmon, which I hate, paired with asparagus, which I hate more. Thankfully there is rice pilaf, which I love. I serve myself the smallest sliver of salmon, one stalk of asparagus, and a huge mound of rice.

Dad glances at my plate as I slide into my chair and laughs. "Carb loading?" he jokes.

"Yes. Thanks for the cover, Dad."

I pick up my fork as my mom looks at my plate disapprovingly but says nothing. She stabs a piece of asparagus on her plate and sets it on mine.

"So, can we meet this young woman?" Dad asks.

"You mean meet Alli?" I mumble, a piece of rice escaping from my mouth. "Sure."

After dinner I text Alli.

My parents want to say hi. Can you come in before we go?

An hour passes before I get a response.

Sure. I get it.

* * *

ALLI

After Brandon texted that his parents want to meet me, I spend extra time choosing my outfit for tonight and putting on makeup.

I step around the pile of discarded clothes next to my bed and walk out wearing a short, green dress with white stripes from the Gap and the gray Allbirds my dad got me for Christmas last year.

Two hours and two (okay, three) warm cookies after my mom and Ray left for their Italian dinner, I'm in my stepdad's silver Audi sedan. In the back seat, I've stashed a flimsy paper plate loaded with a dozen chocolate chip cookies covered by aluminum foil.

I stick Brandon's address into Waze, and it guides me to his address in ten minutes.

As I turn into his driveway, I admire his family's pretty stone house, with a thin band of ivy trellising down the front. I park behind his dad's white Chevy Traverse and step out.

When I squeeze between the two cars, I can see a small sticker, red, blue, gold, and white, affixed to the right corner of the Chevy's rear window. On it are the words *National Rifle Association* encircling an Eagle that grasps a gun in each talon.

Brandon swings open the front door. He's wearing a purple V-neck T-shirt that strains against his (*sigh*) perfect chest. He bounds down the porch steps.

"Hey," he says, stopping inches in front of me.

He notices I've trained my eyes on the NRA logo.

"Yeah, these are my dad's wheels. You know, Second Amendment shit. My dad's a bit obvious about it, huh?" he remarks casually.

"You think?" My mind whirls with what this means about Brandon, too.

"My parents are inside. It'll just take a minute." Brandon grasps my hand and guides me gently inside. There is an overstuffed, brown-tweed sofa across from a huge television set mounted above the fireplace. The top shelf in their built-in bookcase holds a small wine rack stacked with what appear to be identical bottles of red wine topped by gold foil, which seems out of place to me. I've never been somewhere where a case of wine has such a position of prominence.

Framed family photos completely overwhelm a dark wooden table nearby. One of them jumps out to me right away: Brandon and his dad dressed in full camouflage, standing in front of a small, green tent and smiling broadly into the camera.

Brandon's mom walks toward me and extends her hand. "Hi. I'm Nancy. It's great to finally meet you. Brandon has told us so much about you. And your swim scholarship. Congratulations on that achievement," she adds sweetly.

Then she drops my hand and takes off her glasses, which she wipes on the fabric of her long, green skirt. She has cropped brown hair with streaks of gray and crinkle lines alongside her mouth when she smiles. She looks a lot older than my mom, like either she spent too much time in the sun or grew up somewhere crazy hot, like Florida or maybe Arizona. Or she could just be old, like sixty maybe.

Next, Brandon's dad steps closer and pumps my hand up and down. "Stanley," he says with a friendly smile. "It was my dad's name, too. Brandon thanks me every day he isn't Stanley the third." I laugh. He looks old, too. Balding and paunchy, his tailored shirt straining at the buttons.

When I take back my hand, I know I should say something like, "I like your house," or "Stanley's a great name." But I'm distracted by the books next to the television set. One is titled *In Trump We Trust* by Ann Coulter. I know all about Ann Coulter's politics. She went to college with my very Republican uncle, Ron, who loves to tell and retell the story about when she had walked up to him in a history class and complimented one of the editorials he'd written for the Cornell student newspaper. My dad stays far away from talking politics, but his brother has always been a proud and loud Republican.

Brandon takes my hand again and smiles, but he seems uneasy at my lack of small talk.

"Well, it's nice to meet you," I say and then glance at Brandon.

"I won't be too late," he says, as together we walk out the door. Brandon slams it behind us.

"You weren't too friendly," he says cautiously, letting go my sweaty palm. "Is something wrong?"

"Maybe. I don't know," I stammer, searching for the best way to move my thoughts forward.

"Do your parents watch Fox News?" I ask as we stand at the end of his front walkway.

"Actually, it's kinda all they watch, to be honest. That and the History Channel," answers Brandon.

"Don't you think that's a problem?"

"Whoa, Alli. Are you calling out my parents because they aren't liberal like you are? That's not fair."

"It's just that was a lot for me to take in. And I saw that photo of you and your dad in camo. Were you out hunting? I didn't realize your family is so gun crazy."

"Alli, it's not like that. I go deer hunting with my dad once a year in Wisconsin. We have a few guns in a safe. They're locked up. It's not a big deal."

"But it *is* a big deal."

"Look, I don't know what to say to make all this go away between us. Can we just let it go, at least for tonight? Okay?"

I scrunch up my forehead as I process this information.

"You do realize, in Florida, there was a bad guy with a gun but no good guys to stop him. Right?"

Brandon looks at me and shakes his head. "Alli, I don't have all the answers. I'm tired. I like you, but this is who I am. This is my family. You have to get along with them if we're hanging out."

"I'm sure they're great," I say. I realize I've just ambushed him about the people he loves the most. "I mean, they are your parents. They sound badass, being in the Marines and all. I didn't give them a chance tonight, did I?"

Brandon shakes his head and pouts. Right now, he is protecting his parents from his judgy, know-it-all girlfriend. And I don't want to be that person. My mind whirls with competing thoughts. I shake my head and imagine them spilling out then vanishing into thin air.

"So, are we good?" he asks.

"Yes, we're good. Sorry, I just was thrown for a minute." I flash a weak smile. "We're more of an ESPN family. Not much politics talk in our house. So, this is all new to me. I don't think I made a good impression, though."

His front door opens and his mom peeks her head outside, studying us curiously. "Hi, kids," she says tentatively. "I hope everything is okay?"

"Mom, we're just talking. Please go inside," Brandon answers brusquely. His tone urges her to make a hasty retreat. She waves at us and backs up to shut the door.

"And that didn't help," I admit.

"C'mon, there's always second impressions."

We walk over to the car and climb in opposite doors.

"Man, I smell cookies," Brandon says, excited. "Psych!"

* * *

BRANDON

Philip had texted Alli earlier to let herself in. When we open the front door to his house, I follow her and her plate of cookies inside and up to a second-floor door.

As we trudge up the staircase to the attic, she cautions, "Be careful on these steps."

Hanging tightly onto the banister, we scale a set of rickety wooden stairs that squeak with each step. We arrive in a room ablaze with light. Three guys sit on a dirty coach, while Danielle and Jodi sit across from them on oversized pillows strewn about the floor.

I hear a chorus of "Heys" and a few half-waves go around the room.

"Hey, guys, my brothers helped me with the cookies today," Alli says as she drops the plate heavily in the middle of the table with half-empty beer bottles around its edges.

"That sounds a bit dangerous, but I'll take my chances." Phil crumples the sheet of aluminum foil from on top of the plate and chucks it at Jamael.

"What are you guys doing?" I ask, eyeing playing cards stacked in small piles on the table. "Are you playing Shithead?"

"Yeah, man, and Damian is almost shit. You guys can jump in the next game." Alli and I slide down next to each other on the pillows at the end of the table.

"My parents like to play that," I say, "but they call it Palace."

"That's what us proper folk call the game," Jodi chimes in, raising her voice up a snooty octave.

I nod at her perfect pitch. "Exactly! Are you good at this?" I ask, turning to Alli.

"What do you think?" she teases. "I beat these guys in everything. Except chess. Phil is the master."

Phil glances up from the spread of cards fanned out in his hand. "It's true. I may be the chess savant, but Alli has some secret Connect Four strategy that wins every time. And don't get me started on her flipping Jenga magic."

Alli flashes me a broad, knowing smile. I squeeze her thigh.

"I am learning that, too. When we played Jenga, I didn't have a chance," I say slyly. Alli laughs about the secret only we share.

Two hours in, she yawns as we lock eyes. It's such a downer to shut down a night before 11:30 when you're eighteen, but I know she's had a huge day.

"Hey, guys, we're heading out," she tells the group as I stand up and extend my hand to help her rise from the mushy pillow she's parked on. "I was up at 5 a.m. for swim practice today."

"You're a masochist, Alli. We're just getting started," says Phil, as he grabs an iconic guitar from its perch next to the TV.

I'm actually glad we're heading out, as Guitar Hero is not my jam.

Alli and I settled back in the car, bullshitting about the night as she drives toward my house, when she chooses to change the subject.

"Hey, you were honest with me about your parents and their politics. I appreciate that. I have to be honest with you about something, too. It's something good."

"Okay," I say. "What's up?"

"This is the first night Ray's let me drive his Audi since June. He knows I just hate driving mom's minivan with Goldfish crackers all over the floor."

"Sure, I would, too."

"Well, I got a ticket in Ray's car when I was driving downtown to see my dad after he got robbed. I just wasn't myself, and I turned the wrong way onto a one-way street, and guess what's right in front of me?"

"Shit. Did you hit a car?"

"No. But a cop car was, like, right there. He flashes his lights and does that siren thing. I was already a mess from my dad's stuff, so I just pulled over and started crying. The cop gave me a ticket. He barely said a word, just took my license, gets in his car, and comes back ten minutes later with my license and a $150 ticket. Ray and my mom had to pack up my brothers in the minivan to come down and get me, because I was such a wreck and couldn't stop crying to drive home," Alli says, rambling on. "My mom had promised me that, senior year, I would have a midnight curfew, but because of my fuck-up, that didn't happen. And I was banned from his car. But all of a sudden, he's decided to be Mr. Nice Guy, so here we are. I get to drive his car *and* stay out till midnight."

"But it's only 11:30." I point to the clock on the dash.

"I know. I had a long day. But I won't get home till 11:45 after I drop you off. That's something, right?"

She pulls into my driveway and shuts off the engine.

"True. I'm just glad you made it to the other side."

"I did." She turns to face me.

I move closer, and we kiss, our tongues eager to explore further. I press my body tightly against hers. I want so much more time with her tonight to fool around and hang out, just the two of us. I slide my hand over her shirt to caress her right breast.

Alli sharply pulls back and puts her hand on my chest to create some distance.

"I still think we have things to talk about. But not tonight. I'm tired and a bit confused."

"About us?" I ask, fear creeping into my voice.

"Maybe I just need to sleep. I want to think about things when I'm not so tired."

"Okay. Whatever you want." Deflated, I switch to my game face. "I'm glad you met the parents. They are great, and I think you should get to know them more."

Alli touches my shoulder as I'm about to get out of the car. "You're one hundred percent right to ask that of me. I just have to figure out if I can do all this."

Her words sting. I get that she's tired, but she has no right to make me feel like her charity case, when I've been nothing but honest about who I am. I propel myself farther away from her and slam the car door shut as I jump out. I'm mad on so many levels right now. I'm especially pissed that the real world keeps creeping into dates with my girlfriend and completely fucks up what should have been another epic night burning with perfect chemistry.

* * *

ALLI

Simone's room is one of my favorite places to hang out. She has this queen-sized bed with, seriously, ten pillows in all different shapes and sizes... round, square, and rectangular... each one encased in a purple or fuchsia pillowcase.

"This is the girliest bed I've ever seen," I blurted out the first time I set foot in her room, back when we were eleven-year-old middle schoolers.

"I know, isn't it great?" she answered in all seriousness.

Right away, I'd questioned what this girl in my swim club who embraced so much *pink* could possibly have in common with me, besides the fact that we both were fierce swimmers on the same club team and lived close enough for our families to carpool to practices and meets.

When I first took in the overkill of colorful pillows atop a soft, green bedspread dotted with colorful flowers, I was convinced we'd never be great friends.

The more I got to know Simone, though, the more I realized the flashy decor totally fit her badass personality and I had a lot to learn from her self-confident swagger.

Simone has proudly embraced both her inner diva and the fact that she is a ruthless contender in the pool. She loves to shine. She loves the limelight. And that means winning. But she also loves to surround herself with bold colors and gravitates toward anything ruffled, sparkly, or bright. (All three is her trifecta!) And that quickly became one of my favorite things about her. She brings so much light into my life.

Today, her bedspread is a splotch of purple and blue. I burrow myself under the covers, drowned by the pillows.

"Talk to me," she says, sitting atop her bedspread and rearranging three pillows to support her back.

"Oh, Simone." I sigh. "I think Brandon and I are not gonna work out."

"No way, José." I smile at her attempt to make me laugh.

"Yes way, Simone. There's too much different shit between our families. It's stuff that's not okay. I mean, Brandon's parents are gun nuts and watch Fox News. Maybe Brandon is like that, too."

"What's his parents' philosophy on Black Lives Matter? That's what I want to know." Simone slides down so she is lying next to me.

"Simone. Black Lives Matter is not a deep philosophical battle. It's a thing people just support. Don't make me more of a headcase about this."

"Well, all I know is you keep complaining about Brandon and his family and his politics. So, what am I supposed to say? You shouldn't just assume these things."

"I'll ask him, but I don't expect any surprises." I turn to her, hopeful. "I told him I would be less judgmental about how our politics clash. But it's hard."

"Then just get past it. I mean, you're not marrying Brandon."

"I know I promised you I was going to chill out."

"So, do it then."

"Just like that?"

"Yes. Just like that. Now enough about you," she says, adding, "Let me tell you about my problems."

I rest my head against a deep-purple silk pillow and tune in to my best friend. She grabs her laptop from next to her bed and, after a few clicks, shows me a long, cotton-candy-pink dress on the screen.

"I can't decide, but I think I like this more than the sapphire blue one," she states matter-of-factly. "But now, Darryl says he won't wear a pink bowtie. That he's already ordered a tux with a blue one to match my dress. Like, really? He can't change a *tie*? Please."

I peek at the dress image Simone has pushed inches from my face.

"Simone, no. I can't let you wear that dress. Darryl is right. Go with the blue one," I say in all honesty. This dress is slim-cut and floor-length with a hem that pools into a small train and a plunging V-neck held up with rhinestone spaghetti straps.

"I love this dress!" Simone wails, pointing to the screen.

"If you wear this dress, I'm going to have to wear sunglasses to look at you," I kid. "And that will ruin the look I'm going for. Not to mention, you'll kill yourself walking with all that fabric at your heels."

She closes her laptop and shakes her head. "Now I don't know which of you is more boring."

"I know. Just text Darryl he owes me one, okay?" As she smiles, I thrust her phone into her hands.

* * *

BRANDON

Sorry things got so messy last night. Are you free to grab a snack with me?

"Yes. I just put my clothes in the dryer. Where?

It's my treat. A surprise. I'll pick you up at 2 in the Audi.

If this is Alli's way of apologizing via text, it's not a bad start.

An hour later, she pulls her dad's car into a parking spot in front of the last place on Earth I thought we would end up.

"I am so happy right now," she says minutes later, as we sit across from each other in a booth at McDonald's, sharing an order of large fries.

"I can't believe it," I say, taking a sip from my large Sprite. "I never thought this kinda food would be your thing."

"Just the fries. And the mango smoothie. Though I only do it once in a while." Alli pauses and stares thoughtfully into the distance. Then she catches my eye and smiles shyly. "Well, to be honest, probably like once a week. The sugar in here is a killer." I notice she's already slurped down a quarter of her smoothie. "But so fricking good. You know?"

I nod. I *do*! "I'll leave the rest of the fries to you. My dad is grilling steaks for dinner. I saw them marinating in the fridge, and they are pretty huge. That's his signature dish. Steak, baked potato, broccoli. I think he makes *that* once a week."

"*Hmmm*," Alli says, considering. "About your parents. I thought about what you said last night. I've been harsh on them. I'm sorry. One of the reasons I wanted us to talk today face-to-face is so I can ask you a question. Ready?"

I nod slowly, not liking where this is going.

She takes a deep breath and then lets the air out slowly. "Okay. Well. I'm the girl who is asking you to come to the March for Our Lives rally on Saturday in Chicago. A march against gun violence. Against all this senseless killing. Not just in the schools but everywhere. In Chicago, people are dying just walking to school. Or playing in the park."

After she asks, she sits straight up and dips her head to one side, as though waiting for me to jump on board.

"I care about what's happening on our streets too, but I don't want to fix it the same way you do. Gun laws can also deny good people the right to protect themselves," I say without hesitation. "I didn't go to the one last month, and now nothing has changed for me. It's not where I'm comfortable."

"Well, that's the thing. I talked to Simone."

"Uh-oh, that doesn't sound good." I wait for the rest.

"She made me realize that you and I both are overreacting to everything in our orbit. But what if we just *react*? You know, not overreact… Smart, huh?"

"Simone said that?"

"She just clarified for me that we can do this different. Or is it differently? One of those."

Yeah, both sound okay to me.

"She also wants me to ask you about Black Lives Matter," she adds quietly.

"*Huh*. What about it?" I ask, my voice rising. "I mean, I get that racism is a huge problem and we all need to be part of the solution."

"Well, do you talk about this with your parents?"

"Yeah. I've heard them argue about it. My mom is not happy with players kneeling at football games during the national anthem. She says it disrespects our flag and everyone who serves our country.

Then my dad tells her taking a knee is their choice to make. So..." I lean further into the conversation. "I like what Tom Brady said. 'You gotta respect what people are going through.'"

I straighten my back against the hard-plastic booth and wait for Alli's next move.

"I don't mean to grill you. Sorry. It's just I'm thinking about these issues for the first time. This is all new territory for me. I've never voted before. In the next election, I'm definitely going to vote, even though I'll be really busy in college."

"That feels so far away though. Why are you thinking about that now?" I ask her.

"We need to make sure our priorities are counted. You can't do that sitting on the sidelines." She puts out her pinky for us to pinky swear. "To us voting." I link pinkies with her, although it's stupid and corny. It's not that I won't follow through. It's just nowhere on my current radar.

Alli edges closer and takes hold of my outstretched hand. "I'm going to a sign-making meeting tomorrow after school in the cafeteria that Justine is organizing. Why don't you come and make a sign that says what you believe in? Make that part of the scene at Saturday's march. Have your words out there with mine."

I feel cornered and slowly pull my hand back. "I don't want to be part of something that makes me feel like a bad guy just because I don't believe every last gun should be thrown into the fire and melted down."

"See. That's overreacting. Let's try reacting instead..."

"I get what you're saying. But I'm not sure I want to be out there, even with you."

"Sleep on it. I'll text you the deets for the sign-making. You decide."

"You can text it to me, but probably not gonna happen. So, I have news. Charlie and I are set as roommates. We put in the housing request. It's done."

"That's so great. I'm happy for you. I have a big meet I need to get serious about. I've been slacking. That's my news. Not as good. But I'm going to get refocused. I got a bit off track, and it's showing in my training times."

I peer down at the greasy napkins on the table between us. One lone French fry is left. I look at Alli, to see if she wants it.

"All yours," she says.

"If you insist." I pop the salty fry into my mouth.

Later that night, after dinner and a Bulls game on the sofa with Dad, where they lost miserably to the New York Knicks, I decide to test the waters.

"Dad, there's a march on Saturday in Chicago. It's kinda about Parkland but also about guns. I don't think I should go. But some of my friends want me to."

"Would you jump off a building if your friends asked you to?"

"Ha-ha. This is a bit more realistic, right?"

"True," he says matter-of-factly. "But my point is, don't be a follower. Blaze your own path. My son is not going to stand around chanting with a bunch of kids whose parents didn't fight to keep this country safe. And it takes guns to do that. Don't forget that. Guns have secured your safety. Your security and the security of everybody in this great nation."

"Okay. I get it."

"Good. Just keep your head down and do what's right." My dad stands up. "I'm going to walk Astor. Good night." He pats my shoulder, and I look into his face as we share a smile.

As he walks away, I text Alli.

I can't go to the march Saturday. Or your sign making. Sorry. Let's do something else though. This weekend.

The phone rings and I click on it to hear Alli's voice before I even get to say hey. "This march is important to me. And my boyfriend should be there. It's just too much for me to know you want to skip it." She pauses. Silence. Then, softly, she adds, "This is shitty. I keep trying to make this work, but I don't know if we belong together."

"Alli. We do. Belong together. We're going to prom. We have so much fun together. Don't let this end what we have. There's no problem between us. I'm the same person."

"Yes. But things feel different now."

"That makes no sense to me," I say, wanting her to understand that we are good. That things are still good. "I had a great time with you today."

"It just seems broken between us. I want to stand up for something, and you could care less. I know your mom and dad don't approve of me anyway."

"This is only about you and me. And we're the same people we've always been. I'm the same Brandon then and now."

"I know that. I do."

"This is crazy." I shake my head at how she's responding to my yearning to save what we have.

"Maybe so. I need to think. I guess overreacting wasn't the issue. The problem is we don't want the same things."

"I want us to work through this," I say, my voice getting almost shaky with the passion I feel for her. "There must be a middle ground we can both agree on."

"I don't see one," she says firmly. "You believe in the right for people to have guns. But I have a right not to be around guns. I gotta go."

I stand with the phone still at my ear. Now there's only silence on the other end.

* * *

ALLI

After practice, Cam calls me aside.

"Hey, Alli, how are you feeling? Are you ready for Junior Nationals?"

"*Um*, you know I am. Why are you asking me that?"

"I really want this meet to go well for you. Your Miami-Ohio coach called me yesterday. He's concerned about your times from the Senior Championship a few weeks ago. He asked me if you were injured. I told him you are dealing with some stress right now. It's all this time and energy you're putting into this new club you're involved with. Am I right?"

"Did my dad tell you that?" Coach nods his head. I scrunch my forehead, trying to figure out how mad I need to be at my dad right now. Deep down, I know I deserve more of a chewing out than Coach is giving me. That my performance in the pool lately has been disappointing, and I've been letting down the whole team.

Coach Cam and my dad can blame it on my full to-do list. I'll never admit out loud how it's really this uncertainty with Brandon that's messing with my brain. One minute, I harden my heart to him and we're done, over, kaput. The next, my mind conjures up an image, like the one of us together on Valentine's Day morning, where he was waiting for me outside my graphic arts class, and I cave like a ball of mush.

Uh-oh. My brain spirals. That's bad, if a college coach is worried about my times. "I guess I have been a bit distracted. I promise I'll go big this weekend. I know I can do it." I rush the words so they almost stick together as I speak, hoping to smooth this over quickly. "I'll swim over spring break, if you think it'll help. Not take the week off like I was planning to."

"I think that would be a good idea. I'll design some training sets for you to work on that week. It wasn't like you, messing up your flip turn at the Senior meet. In all the years you've been swimming, I've never seen you miss the wall in competition before," he says.

"I don't know what came over me. Why I flipped early. It won't happen again. I'll be here every day during spring break," I say. "Just *please* don't add dry-land training to my long sets. You know how much I hate that."

"I can't make any promises. But good for you. That's the Alli I know. Now, let's get to work. Warm up with a 500 easy freestyle. Then move to a 500-pyramid set."

"Got it."

I dive in the water and launch straight into fly. As I approach the wall, I do what comes naturally and time my flip turn, so I push off the wall with a great force that propels my body deep into the pool. I've got to do every one of my turns just like this at Junior Nationals. No mistakes allowed. I've worked too long and too hard to have a college coach question if I'm D1 material.

Junior Nationals is only the next hurdle I must overcome to prove I'm worthy of this scholarship spot. After that, I need to keep my head in the game for four more years. That's a shit-ton of flip turns!

* * *

BRANDON

When I walk into the kitchen, my mom's there with her jacket on and her purse on the counter, ready to go to the swim dinner. I'm glad she's cued up to do this, but as I get closer to her, I start to question if this is gonna be a good idea.

Mom's fingers hold a glass of red wine. I hope it's her first glass of the night. I know better than to ask. So, I do what I've always done. I make the only choice there is. I ignore it and focus on me. Not her messiness but mine.

"Mom, I need to tell you one thing. And ask you something."

"Okay, what's up."

"Well, Alli and I got in a fight. We may be broken up. I don't know. So, it could be a bit awkward at my club team award night. We are kinda in a weird place."

"Okay. I'm sure you will figure out what is best for you." She walks over to the sink and gently rinses the half-empty wine glass under the faucet, then sticks it in the dishwasher. When she steps back over to me, we are standing side by side.

"What do you want to ask me?"

"Well, that's the thing. I don't want to blow it up or anything, but can we take your car tonight?"

"I guess so. I don't understand."

"Alli's just a bit upset by Dad's NRA bumper sticker. Can we not go into it? Just trust me."

"Oh. Well, okay. Sure. I see. No problem, Brandon. I don't want to make anyone who doesn't support the NRA uncomfortable."

"Mom. She really hates guns. Her dad was robbed in his pawnshop. At gunpoint. She thinks maybe we shouldn't go to prom together."

"Oh, Brandon. That is awful. Completely terrible. I am so sad to hear that. Maybe you need to ask a girl to go to prom with you, though, who doesn't have baggage."

"This isn't baggage, Mom."

"Okay, that's a bad word. But if she's out of step with our family's values and she disrespects your beliefs, then maybe she isn't the right person for you."

"Mom, you are not in a relationship with Alli. I am. Or I may be. And we are not talking about this again. Just don't drive that car tonight. Okay? That's all I'm asking you and dad."

"There's no need to get yourself all worked up. We'll take my car. Don't worry. I think your dad has a client dinner in Rosemont tonight anyway."

I look at her and hope she didn't have more than half a glass of wine.

"Why don't I drive over there, Mom. Would that be okay?" I ask, tentatively.

She grabs her bag. "Yes. Yes, why don't you drive."

I exhale inside, glad to have vanquished that hurdle. Still. I'm worried.

* * *

ALLI

Mom and I stand outside the front door of my high school, watching my dad walk quickly our way. I wave enthusiastically while she opens her purse and drops her phone inside.

Dad and I hug, and Mom gives him a tight wave.

"Hi, Steven," she says tersely.

"Good to see you, Janice," he answers, his voice warm and welcoming.

We open the doors to the school's main entrance and walk down the hallway to the cafeteria. Inside the smaller staff cafeteria, long wooden tables are sprinkled with confetti and decorated with green foam blocks stuck through with rainbow-colored pinwheels.

Twizzlers, Sweethearts, lollipops, and about five other types of candy are piled around the foam centerpieces. Junk-food heaven, some would call it. I'm surprised Kaitlyn okayed this mess. At an event to celebrate our athletic achievements, it's not cool to be greeted by this cavity-inducing sugar overload. Still. I'll embrace the vibe someone put time into setting up here. I love Twizzlers, so that part they did get right at least.

I walk over to the food table and plop down our bag of tortilla chips, find a little space, and then open up the jar of Frontera salsa.

I hurry back to my parents, who stand awkwardly next to each other, not talking.

Brandon walks in with his mom, Nancy, and beelines over my way.

"Hey," he says, then turns to my mom. "Hi, Mrs. Nixen."

"Oh, it's nice to see you, Brandon," she says. "This is Steven, Alli's dad."

Dad turns to Brandon and seems to quickly size him up. Brandon sticks out his hand and my dad pumps it enthusiastically. "I've heard a bit about you, Brandon. Glad you're Wisconsin-bound. A great school."

"Thank you," Brandon replies. "Mom, these are Alli's parents." She turns from greeting another swim parent, and introductions go all around.

"Nice to meet you," my mom says. "Our children have become quite the item."

"Brandon, we're an item!" I exclaim a little too loudly, embarrassed by my mom's outburst. He laughs and cocks his head to one side. I get how he's surprised I haven't filled in my mom on the latest—that Brandon and I are not exactly "an item" right now. That we're basically "on hold."

"Well, I think they have jumped into this relationship a bit quickly," Nancy adds, looking over at her son. "After all, they do have some issues they differ on that are fundamental."

My mom looks confused. "What do you mean fundamental?"

"I just don't want to see my son compromise who he is. That's all. I think it is nice they are spending time together, but Brandon does seem to have changed recently. He's been harder for me to talk to. We'll eventually work it out, but I am concerned."

"Oh, well, I know these kids have their phases. I'm sure, if you trust in his judgement, all will be fine."

"Maybe." Nancy hesitates, turning to her son to rub his back very publicly. "Should we get some food, Brandon?"

* * *

BRANDON

Reluctantly, I follow my mom over to the long table covered with green plastic and overloaded with foods that just don't go together. Pasta salad, chips and salsa, deviled eggs, mini-meatballs smothered in a mystery sauce and speared with toothpicks, potato chips, dill pickles. Next to a huge cake decorated like a swimming pool sits a blue Jell-O mold with thin banana slices floating inside. It's clever, as it reflects our club colors, blue and white, but at the same time: gross.

I take another moment to try to calm myself down before I respond, but I don't succeed. "What the fuck, Mom? What was that?" I fume angrily as I slap a spoon of pasta salad onto a thin paper plate.

She stares at me with a frown. "Language, Brandon. Do not speak to me like that. This is another example of what I just said. You are emotional and irrational around Alli."

I want to stew in these juices. I'm pissed. But this is no place to start a scene. I reel it in. I realize she thinks she's protecting me. But she didn't follow the script, either.

"Mom, Alli makes me happy," I say, taking down my tone. "I like her a lot. I don't need you to make things more complicated for us. Just don't do it, okay?"

She nods and quickly walks over to the other side of the table, where she grabs a paper plate and starts to fill it with offerings from the bounty of dishes. "We'll discuss this later," she says sharply. "Let's enjoy our evening." She takes her full plate and walks over to an empty table to sit down. I follow and plunk down noisily beside her.

I peek over at Alli, who is sitting two tables over, with her mom. I shrug. "Sorry," I mouth, shaking my head.

She nods slightly and turns away to talk to Simone's mom. While her back is to me, our table slowly fills in with Alma, Malcolm, and their parents. And that's how we spent the next hour—surrounded by our senior teammates and families but gazing at opposite sides of the room.

During the awards-night presentation, led by seniors Ainsley and Noam, Alli gets the "Eat My Dust" Paper Plate award, while I'm saddled with the "Biggest Quitter" award, which I guess I deserve. Simone seems happy with her "YOLO" award, even though I feel like it says nothing about her being a kickass swimmer. We all chipped in to buy Coach Cam a framed photo of us seniors decked out in navy-blue Dolphin sweatshirts, and a water bottle with the phrase "These are the tears of my swimmers" emblazoned on it, which led to a huge belly laugh for a full ten seconds before his announcement that he would "use it every day."

As the event wraps up, I'm standing next to Coach as he and Mom reminisce about the time I was cheering for my relay after my leg and I slipped off the edge of the pool, falling into the opposing team's lane. My first and only DQ. I fake smile while the two of them laugh too loudly about my stupid stumble—and then I notice Alli leaving with her mom and dad.

She sends me a text as she heads out the door:

We're off. Talk later.

And I think, *Shit, that's cold.* But I play along as she keeps her distance from me and my mom and give a thumbs-up to her text.

I want to push away the thought trying to wedge itself into my head all night. That mom had wine before she came here. Just a half glass. That's all I saw, at least. But the way she jumped down my throat tonight, I'm pretty sure she drank more than that. Still, policing Mom is not my job. I've got nothing to tell Dad about, right?

I grab both our jackets to signal to her I want to leave. She is still talking to Coach Cam. I walk up and thrust her jacket at her, and she abruptly grabs it from my hands. She makes her apologies to Coach

Cam about needing to leave and then huffs out the door in front of me. That's my mom being true to herself, something she has always done.

What a mess tonight ended up being. I have made two women angry, and I've done nothing to deserve any of it. The problem is, here we are, all being ourselves and all staring out at the world from different corners of it. So, where does that leave me and Alli?

* * *

ALLI

Later that night, as I'm lying in bed about to fall asleep, my phone rings. Brandon glows bright on the screen.

"Hi. Fun award night, huh?" I say.

"More like shitty. I hated how my mom acted. But you have to understand where she comes from. She's old school."

"I just don't want to be with someone I fight with. I don't know if we're good together," I say flat out.

"Wait. Let's not decide this way. Can't we talk about it in person?" Brandon pleads.

"We've talked. Remember? Too much."

"Yeah, but you've been upset, I'm upset. Let's take some time to calm down. Can I come by? Maybe tomorrow night?"

"Fine," I answer. "After dinner. I'll be home."

Seconds later, he responds. "Great. I'll text you."

"Okay. See you then." I click the phone off and turn back to bury my cheek in my fluffy pillow.

We can't keep on this way, going in circles. Something has to change. At least now, we have an expiration date on this uncertainty. Tomorrow will decide our future and if we will have one together.

* * *

BRANDON

"Mom, after dinner, I need to use the car. Is that okay?"

"To see Alli?"

"Yeah. Why?"

"I just think everyone in our family should share our same values. I've raised you to understand that. Just because you like a girl doesn't mean you adopt her liberal ideology. I need you to think for yourself. To remember you are the son of two United States Marines who fought for this country, for liberty."

"Mom, you're putting me in the middle of this impossible situation. Can you please just pull back? For me?"

"I don't want to talk about this any further. In fact, I'm going to rest for a while. Can you manage dinner? There's some spaghetti and sauce in the pantry. And check the freezer—maybe we have some frozen green beans and meatballs or something." She walks over to the kitchen counter, grabs the half-full wine bottle from the kitchen counter, and fills her glass. As she tips it to her lips, she shuffles toward the stairs, heading up to what I know will be her darkened bedroom.

Both my parents served in Desert Storm during the Gulf War. My mom did one tour of duty in Saudi Arabia. She served in a platoon with thirty men and a few other women; she went three months without a proper shower and slept on top of her HMMVY for a week straight. She watched a Marine die from nerve-gas poisoning. My dad spent two tours in Kuwait. He has recounted to me many times the firefights he engaged in against Iraqi troops.

Dad tells us that's why, when mom gets angry or stressed, she goes into zombie mode. It's something only people who've experienced what he calls "the underbelly of a war" can truly understand.

She just grabs for a bottle of wine and checks out until the emotions pass. Then she engages like all is okay and eventually disengages again when she realizes the problem hasn't disappeared. She's gone to counseling for many years, but by now, she's owned it. It's just her way to cope with stress. Dad calls it her PTSD issue.

What he doesn't understand is it becomes *our* issue, too. Nobody wants to upset Mom, none of us want to make waves in the house, because of the tsunami of sadness it ushers in. But we have our own shit to go through, so sometimes it cannot be helped. I should have seen this coming. The signs were there, and I purposely pushed them aside, not wanting to see that I've opened up the door to her cray-cray.

I cannot live through three more weeks of my mom's wild mood swings. And prom pictures will be a nightmare. I can't have my parents in the same room as Alli's. This is just too messed up to believe.

I have to tell Alli we can't go back and forth anymore. That it's too exhausting. Too hard on my parents. Well, mostly on my mom. I need to let Alli go and just enjoy being a second-semester senior. Can we put this all behind us and move into a new phase? Where we are not boyfriend and girlfriend, just friends?

Dad and I eat a quiet dinner of spaghetti and green beans. I couldn't find any meatballs, so this meal basically sucks. I left a plate of food by Mom's door before we sat down to eat, and, if past experience tells me anything, it's still sitting there.

"Can I take the car after dinner to hang out with Alli?"

"How's the homework and final studying going?" he asks, looking over at me with his spaghetti-laden fork suspended in midair.

"Dad, I'm a second-semester senior. You don't have to worry about me. I've got it covered."

"Okay, just a few hours. It's still a school night," he adds before devouring the spaghetti from his fork. After a few minutes of our forks clicking on plates as we sit across the table from each other, wrapped up in our own heads, Dad cracks through the veneer.

"Mom's in one of her moods tonight. I'm worried about her. Before dinner, I found her sitting under the covers in bed, drinking her glass of wine, with a closed book on her lap. She was just gazing off into space."

"Are you serious? Has she done that before?"

"Not in a long time. But you know your mom. She's a survivor. She'll be fine. I turned on an episode of *International House Hunters.* You know how she loves that show."

"Maybe I should stay here."

"No, go. I'll head up soon and sit with her. She just needs a good night's sleep."

"Okay, Dad. Call me, and I'll come right home. Okay?" Actually, I'm relieved to escape this fragile house for a few hours.

Though, where I'm going will not be any fun, either. Tonight's going to suck. There's no getting around it.

I text Alli.

Can I pick you up to talk?

She texts right back.

KK. 20 minutes.

Twenty-five minutes later, I pull up in front of her house, shooting over a text.

Here.

I watch her emerge from her front door in a short, green dress speckled in white dots. She gives me a quick smile as she glides toward me and the car.

"Let's go hang out at Vanguard Park, okay?" I ask as she settles into the passenger seat and nods her assent. I look over and grin faintly. I try to act chill, even though everything about Alli fires me up. "So, what's going on?" I work hard to keep my voice steady, light.

"Oh, the usual stuff. My brothers are so exhausting. You know how we've had all these huge rains? Ray gives my brothers each a dollar and tells them to go in the backyard and pick up sticks before dinner. I go to check on them after like twenty minutes, and they each have these massive tree branches and start showing off their sword-fighting to me. They are so proud of themselves, and I end up having to break up their duel before someone gets hurt."

"Alli, that sounds like very normal behavior. I mean, they are like eight, right?"

"Boys and their weapons. With everything we've talked about, I really need to explain this to you?"

"I hardly think big sticks even qualify as weapons."

"I mean sticks are not technically weapons, that's true. But they turned them into something dangerous. They could have gotten really hurt. Anyway. What do you want to talk about?"

My phone lights up in the center console. I have a text from mom.

Are you with Alli?

I flick my phone into my right hand before Alli can read it and drive with my left. Guilt starts to wiggle into my head. I think about my mom sitting in bed with a glass of wine because of me. Then I push the image away. I have to focus on Alli. On us. My dad can handle Mom tonight. I have to be present with Alli right now. To say goodbye.

"Is everything okay?" she asks.

"No, it's not. You know that."

"I do. My mom was shocked by how things went down at award night. I told her the whole story. She wants me to ask my camp friend, Sam, to prom. He lives an hour away, but I'm pretty sure he'd come."

"Is that what you want to do?" I ask. I look over at her and notice her eyes are wet, a tear glistening on her cheek.

She shakes her head quickly, her lips pouting.

I drop the phone into my lap and raise my right hand to her cheek, wiping away the tear with my finger.

Without thinking, I touch my finger to my lips and taste her salty tear.

In my lap, I feel my phone buzz. I pick it up and sling it sharply onto the ledge above the car's front dash. I don't want to think about my mom now. Or whoever is bothering me. I want to focus on Alli and what we are losing.

I watch helplessly as the phone bounces off the hard-plastic console, the car's momentum flinging it into the air.

"Oh shit, Brandon," Alli says, as the phone hits her square in the eye. "*Damn it!* Calm down." She pushes away the phone. It bounces on her lap and lands on the floor mat.

She covers her right eye with her hand. "I don't want a black eye in my prom pictures."

"I'm sorry. Really," I say. "That was a dumb move."

We're at the park. I pull over to the curb and turn off the car.

"Are you okay?" I turn to her and lightly brush her hair away from her right eye, relieved to see there's no mark.

"Maybe," she jokes, laughing it off. "Look, it's only prom. I know this is so messy. Maybe I should just take Sam. And you would take...Who would you take?"

"I think I won't go. If I can't go with you," I say. That is the truth, though it is the first time I have actually allowed myself to say it. I haven't wanted to believe it would really happen this way.

"Well then, I guess we should just do that. Switch to Plan B. Can you drive me home? I'm tired. And I may need to ice this baby." She points to her eye.

"Are you mad?" I ask.

"Of course, I'm mad. The whole situation is madness."

"Please don't say that. You know my parents met in the ROTC program at Wisconsin. I've been around guns my whole life. I think we are both just very emotional about things that are important to us." I look at the top of Alli's head as she stares down at her lap.

Silence sits heavy between us.

"I look at you and can't believe you grew up shooting poor defenseless Bambis," says Alli softly, her head still down.

"Oh, that is so unfair. Don't treat me like a criminal. It's called deer season for a reason. It's to help the deer, not hurt them. To control the population, so they don't all die from starvation. I wasn't the one who robbed your dad, so don't put me in the same box as that psycho gun shithead. That really sucks."

Alli raises her face to meet mine. I keep my eyes locked on hers, after I've thrown down words I just couldn't keep bottled up any longer. I know I've upset her, because she abruptly turns her head away from me to stare out the window.

I realize there's nothing more for us to discuss. Alli keeps wanting me to be someone I'm not. I need to accept we've just officially broken up.

I start up the engine, carefully peering into my rearview mirror to check for any cars. Then I start a U-turn to head back down the street the way we just came.

As I turn, Alli reaches down to pick up my phone from where it landed between her feet. I hear a slight crunch.

"Oh, Brandon, no. Your screen's busted. It's all cracked," she moans as she stares at my phone. "I think I stepped on it. Oh man, this is bad."

"*What!*" I screech, knowing how angry my parents are going to be if they have to shell out to fix my iPhone.

I glance over at the gleaming black rectangle in her hand and see a web of white cracks spidering across the dark screen. A panic from all that has gone to shit tonight rises from deep within me and the adrenaline surges straight through my body. Before I realize it, I've stepped too heavily on the gas.

"*Brandon, no! Brandon!*" Alli yells loudly.

I whip my head back to attention and realize I'm staring down a tree that's smack in front of the windshield.

* * *

ALLI

I open my eyes to the sun streaming in through a huge glass window. I spend a minute surveying my situation as my brain focuses on all that surrounds me.

What the hell? Why do I feel like shit? Why am I lying in a hospital bed?

Oh, yeah. Brandon. Last night. *Shit shit shit.*

What is going on?

I look over at my mom and dad, who stand by my bed with red, tired eyes. I'm scared as hell to ask them this question.

"Oh, honey, thank god. You're okay," Mom says gently, as I stare into her weary face. She strokes my hair. Her words and touch are comforting. Her tenderness blankets my soul, and I feel warm. I feel safe.

"I am so tired," I say, testing the waters.

"That's just from the trauma you've been through," Dad explains. "You did sustain a mild concussion, but luckily the airbag lessened the impact. They gave you a brain CT scan after the ambulance brought you in to the emergency room, and thankfully the doctor didn't see any problems."

"So, I'm going to be okay?" I ask. "Everything?"

My mom nods weakly, while my Dad sits unmoving.

"Janice, don't get her hopes up," Dad says. He stoops over and pats the side of my arm.

"What? Dad. What is it?"

"You weren't wearing a seat belt, so you banged your left knee pretty badly." He sounds disappointed, and also a little mad. "They need to do one more test."

"Steven, really. This is not the time," Mom warns. "Honey," she adds, "your dad is concerned about this affecting your swimming. But everything will be fine."

"Mom! That is not fine. That is so not fine." I strain to sit up, but nothing in my body yields. My effort leads nowhere. "You mean my scholarship could be gone? I could lose it?"

My mom and dad look at each other. Then at me. Nobody speaks for a long time.

"We don't know," Dad finally says. "You probably wouldn't lose it. But you might have to redshirt your freshman year. We have to wait for the results of the MRI."

I push that thought away. I refuse to hear my dad's worst-case scenario crap. Instead, I think back to last night. Even with my head feeling woozy, I start to recall exactly how I ended up here.

"How is Brandon? Is he okay?" I ask.

My dad's face gets flushed. "That little shit. Don't get me started."

"The doctor says he's doing well," Mom says, her words tumbling out before my dad can say anything more. "He bruised his nose when the airbag deployed. The person to worry about here is you, Alli. I don't want you to spend a second on that boy. Look what he's done to you."

"Mom." I turn to her, hoping she can be the voice of reason in the room. "You know what he did to me?" I sit up a bit straighter and grab for the edge of the bed with my right hand. My body wants to slump back and rest, but my brain is fired up. I grab the bed frame tighter to stay upright. "He told me to go to prom with Sam. Everything was getting too crazy. And then I think his mom was texting him, and he got mad. His phone broke. It was just an accident. That's all it was."

"You're never seeing that boy again," Dad states coldly as he stares at my legs. "Never. Do you understand?"

"Mom, can you get Dad to calm down? He's freaking me out."

She puts her hand over my dad's as he rests it on the hospital bed frame, which I know can't be easy. Because of my accident, they are now side-by-side in this cold, claustrophobic space, touching the person they used to love. Standing over me and worrying about the only thing the two of them have in common.

I flutter the sheet upward and stare underneath the covers at the black brace on my left leg. It reaches from my calf to my thigh.

"What's up with this?" I ask cautiously.

"That's why they're sending you for an MRI soon. To see," Mom says.

"Because?" I look at my dad. "Dad, why?"

"In the accident, the doctor thinks your knee slammed hard into the glove compartment. It could be a torn PCL."

"What's that?" I ask, trying to process the foreign-sounding initials.

"It might be nothing. Or it could be bad, sweet pea," my dad says. He moves backward to sit next to my bed on the only chair.

"Well, did you Google it?" I know he did. "Can you read it to me?"

Slowly, my dad removes his phone from his back pocket and pulls up the information, details he's probably been researching for hours. He bends forward and reads slowly and sharply, like I'm a child just learning to comprehend words.

> *The posterior cruciate ligament (PCL) is a ligament within the knee. Injuries to the PCL typically occur when the tibia is hit by an outside force while the leg is bent. In general, milder sprains heal within 2 to 4 weeks, but other types of knee sprains may take 4 to 12 months.*

I'm bawling now. I'm flat-out sobbing like a baby. This cannot be. This is not happening. *Possibly four to twelve months? Fuck you, Brandon. How did this all get so fucked up?*

I lean back and every inch of me feels so deeply tired. I nestle into the pillows behind me and will myself to fall asleep. When I wake up, I want to be the Alli I was just twenty-four hours ago, who could jump in the pool and outswim almost anyone, anytime, anywhere.

* * *

BRANDON

I'm wide awake. My face feels like it was hit with a frying pan, like in those old cartoons. But this isn't funny. This is my face, and this is real-life shit. Hours ago, I got up to go to the tiny hospital bathroom, and when I looked in the mirror, what stared back was ugly and deformed. It was me. With a huge, beige bandage over my nose. And a black eye.

Mom and Dad are sitting on chairs in the too-bright, antiseptic hospital room. The morning sun pours in through the oversized window and illuminates their faces. They look wrecked. Pale. Almost as bad as I feel. Nobody is talking. We did that already. They told me the doctors worried I had a concussion. I had tests. I passed. So, now, I'm just fricking Frankenstein. *Woo-hoo!*

My parents wouldn't tell me anything about Alli, just that the doctor told them she hurt her knee "a little bit."

"Can I see her now?" I ask for the third time, knowing she could be down the hall. Maybe even in the room next door.

"I asked the nurse for an update. She did sustain a mild concussion, but everything checked out okay in the CT scan. She told me Alli's going to get an MRI of her knee," Mom answers, droning on.

"Can I text her then? Where's my phone?"

"Where's your phone?" Dad moves to stand over the bed. He's practically screaming as he spits angrily, "*Where's your phone?* Where do you think your phone is? We found it broken on the passenger-side floor mat of your mom's car. Where Alli was sitting. Can you explain that?"

I start to shake. I can't control my trembling body. Tears waterfall from my eyes. I haven't cried like this since I was nine years old and broke my arm falling off the monkey bars. But now I'm very sad. So very scared. Alli is in a hospital bed because of me, and I know I will have to face up to the pain I have caused her.

"I forgot for a minute. I forgot, I forgot," I babble as I pull up the bed sheet to dry my wet cheeks and wipe the snot dripping from my nose. I close my eyes and take a deep breath. Alli comes into focus. I see her smile. I picture her laughing after I handed her the kickboard and asked her to prom. That is the Alli in my mind. But what is the Alli of now? *What did I do?* She must hate me.

"None of this should have happened," Mom says, standing next to me and caressing my right forearm. "You and Alli are not right for each other. This has gone too far."

"Mom, it's not up to you," I wail between sobs, as I continue to wipe my wet face.

I get a grip. She needs to understand what happened last night. "You wanna know why I hit that tree? Because I told her to go to prom with someone else. And I was mad, because she said, when I go deer hunting with Dad, I kill Bambi," I say.

"Brandon, you drove into that tree because you were too emotional about that girl," Mom says. "She's pushing your buttons and setting you off. That is not the girl for you."

"Okay, Mom, whatever you say." I feel crushed by her harsh tone. Her blanket disapproval. I slump down into the bed. She knows me better than I know myself sometimes. I *am* too emotional about Alli. She's hit on a truth I can't deny.

I gaze at her, startled by her drooping posture. By how defeated she looks. I lie back and replay the night in my head. The ugliness that started way before I picked Alli up and we drove to the park.

"Mom," I say, grabbing the controls for the bed to hit the button that raises me up. Once I am mostly vertical, I continue. "I know you had a really tough night last night. Dad told me." I stare at her stricken face. "I didn't want my stuff to become yours. I didn't mean for this—" I stop talking.

My mom abruptly straightens her spine. Her demeanor sharpens in an instant. "Brandon, I have to admit I was in a bad place. But you need me to be strong. This is my reality now." She chooses her words slowly, carefully. "I will not let my demons own me. I realized, after the police called, I have a choice to make. To fall apart or help you and your dad through this. I am tough—I've proven that before—and I need to rely on my strength during times like this. Not get dragged backward." She speaks forcefully while she strokes my arm gently. "This has been a terrible night. But you are my mission, and I choose to accept it."

My dad grabs her free hand. "I'm so proud of you, Nancy," he says. Then, directing his gaze at me, he adds, "Brandon, when I get home, I plan to take the wine bottles out of the house. Mom sees how she's been turning to that a bit too much lately."

"Well, you don't need two patients now, do you?" she says with a weary half-smile. "I'm going to start back at therapy again, too." She grips my dad's hand tightly. "I expect you kids to live with integrity, and that starts with your dad and me showing you every day what that looks like."

The room is silent as I absorb this new normal I have woken up to. I'm not the only mess in the family. We both have some serious healing to do.

"Can I get out of here?" I ask Dad.

"Soon," he says. "Your sister is on her way. She borrowed a friend's car and is driving down from Madison. She's really worried about you."

Finally, some good news. I'm glad she's coming to play buffer between me and my parents. *Thank you, Kelly.*

"Mom, I need to apologize. I have to say sorry to Alli and her parents. Can you make that happen, please?"

She looks at me for an uncomfortable few seconds, her hand resting on my right shoulder.

"Yes. I will," she says. "At least you can try." She turns and slips out the door.

* * *

ALLI

Getting an MRI is spooky. As you lie on a hospital bed, you are slowly sucked into this human-sized tunnel, and then you need to remain completely still while a scanner takes pictures all around your body. It's loud, but there's nothing to do but think.

A constant train of related and unrelated thoughts pop into my brain.

Will the coach pull my scholarship? He better not.

But even if I'm still on the team, I'm going to be behind the curve already. How do I catch up?

How is Brandon? Was this his fault? My fault?

I guess the fault lies somewhere between us. What he wanted from me was something I couldn't give. Or could I? I've basically told him there's only one right answer and that I know it.

Wait! What pull does he have on me that makes me want to defend him, even after all this? It can't be only that he's super-hot. That being touched by him excites every inch of me. Why do I still care about this guy so much?

I like who I am around him. I'm a better version of me. I like that he is confident about who he is but still questioning and searching within himself. He makes me want to walk around more solidly in my own beliefs, but then I'd never considered his as worth discussing.

I haven't let him know any of this. I pushed him away, because it's easier to live in my comfort zone than to listen to him have an opinion that differs from mine and then be forced to form an intelligent response. I wanted him to change without expecting the same from myself.

Maybe Brandon is actually the most self-aware guy I know. I mean, he never turned away from me, but he stood by his values and still wanted to stick by my side. Because of Brandon, I've been challenged to think broadly and deeply for the first time.

Instead of being reactive, I guess I need to be more thoughtful, more open-minded. I...

The MRI machine suddenly whirs open, and the tech helps me down from the table. An orderly comes in to walk me to my room and helps me back into my hospital bed.

After I am settled under the covers, a cheerful nurse with a nametag that reads *Fitzroy* says in a lilting Jamaican accent, "The doctor will be by in a few hours with the results."

"Sure. Thanks," I say, nodding. I close my eyes. A nap sounds good about now. My body and mind are tired from the exertion of too much crying, too much thinking, too much worrying about what this accident has cost me and those who care about me.

* * *

BRANDON

"Oh my god, Brandon!" I hear as the hospital room door flies open. My sister, Kelly, rushes in and skids to a stop at my bedside. She pauses to take in my lumpy form lying in the hospital bed. "My baby brother. Mom was right. You look like hell."

"Thanks, sis. So glad you came all this way to cheer me up."

She rests her arm gently on mine. "How are you? Really?" she asks, concern narrowing her usually wide, sparkling-blue eyes. Her hair is badly bleached; it looks like straw. I'm tempted to call her Scarecrow, but I keep my offensive sibling humor bottled up. I'm sure her frazzled look has more to do with the fact that she chose to commandeer a car and drive two hours, full of worry for her little brother.

"I just want to get out of here," I tell her. "Can you ask when I'm gonna be sprung?"

"The nurse says they're finalizing the paperwork," Mom says from just inside the hospital door. She has a pad of paper in her hand. "Alli's family has asked for privacy while they finish up the tests she needs. I thought maybe you would want to write her a note? We could leave it at the nurse's station for them to deliver to her."

I shake my head, completely relieved I can put the agony of an apology off for a day or, hopefully, more. "It probably was a bad idea, anyway. The meds talking. What am I even going to say to them right now, besides, 'Sorry I'm an asshole'?" I sit up and study the tube connecting my veins to the bag of IV fluids on a pole next to my bed. "Let's go—I feel fine. I need to get out of here."

"You're not an asshole, Brandon," Kelly says. "You just fucked up. Okay, royally fucked up. But it could have been worse. A lot worse." She twists to look behind her. "Sorry, Mom. But I think that word is appropriate right now." Mom nods vigorously.

"But what am I going to do? How can I face Alli and her parents after this shit-show I put us all through?" I grumble. I watch Mom frown, obviously unimpressed I've taken my sister's cue that the door is now wide open to cursing. Considering the situation I'm in, there's no other word that works.

"You don't always need to have a plan. Just breathe, trust, and let go. See what happens," Kelly suggests.

"Wow. Did you just make that up?"

"I wish. I'd be rich *and* famous. It's from Mandy Hale. She's a social media superstar who wrote this bestseller when she was thirty-something. I read some of her stuff for a women, gender, and religion class I took last semester. You know, live your best life, never settle. Oh, and leap before you look. I like that one. Actually, half my class was guys—isn't that funny? I'll get you a copy of her book. You look like you need it now." We sit silently for a few minutes before Kelly continues. "Like, she believes we need to laugh in the face of adversity. So, ha-ha. Isn't this so funny—you're in the hospital," she adds, straight-faced.

I smirk at her attempt to bring some light into my dim reality.

Just then, the nurse walks in and hands my mom the discharge paperwork. "Okay, Brandon. You're good to go," she says. Stepping smoothly in front of my sister, she frees me from the IV then rolls a thin layer of brown antiseptic over the area just inside my elbow and gently applies a sticky bandage.

I am sprung. If there is anything lucky about this situation, it is this. Monday is Day One of spring break, so I have a whole week to hide my black eye and wonky nose from my classmates and figure out a way to apologize to Alli and her parents.

My dad has been sitting quietly in the corner. He bolts up, grabbing his jacket from the back of the chair. He hasn't said a word since my mom left the room. That thirty minutes of silence, when I could close my eyes and let my mind drift into oblivion, is the only good thing that has happened to me today.

This Mandy Hale person may have made a gazillion dollars telling people to laugh awful stuff off, but I cannot imagine how any comedy can come from this situation. There's nothing funny to see here.

* * *

MARCH 30

ALLI

I stand at the kitchen counter, munching on carrot sticks Mom's cut up for me. Since I hurt my knee, she's been acting like my arms are in a brace, too. I do like being the pampered one in the family, though, so there are no complaints from my corner. She's even washed, dried, and folded my laundry *twice* this week.

"Do you think we should put out some food for when they come? Maybe some cheese and crackers?" she asks, crunching on a carrot as I ponder her question.

"Definitely *not*," Ray responds from the kitchen table, where he is sitting with my brothers and their bowls of spaghetti and meatballs. "We are not feeding them anything from this house."

"Okay, okay," my mom says, first loudly and then more softly, trying to calm his storm of words. "I'll put out a pitcher of water and some glasses." She opens a nearby cabinet and pulls out a ceramic pitcher.

Just then, the doorbell rings. Mom and I lock eyes. "I'll get it," I say, hobbling over to the front door and, after taking a deep breath, opening it wide.

"Hi, Dad."

He walks slowly into the room and hugs me tightly. "How's my girl doing?"

"I'm doing so well. The physical therapist says I could be completely out of the brace by May."

"Oh, good, good. Are you keeping up with the therapy exercises at home, too?"

"Yes, I'm following the protocol. You know I want to be ready to swim with my team. It's going to be close, but I think I will be able to at least start training in July. I've lost a lot of muscle mass, so I'm going to have to build that up again."

I know he's bummed I'm missing hell week. But, to be honest, that is the one silver lining of this whole situation. I was so dreading it. Cam tried to put us through a one-week intensive before Christmas Break my sophomore year, but he had to cancel it after two days. One of the guys on the team threw up on the pool deck. Then, my friend Kayla got an overuse shoulder injury during training that sidelined her for the whole winter season.

He sighs big and nods, then lightly squeezes my right shoulder. "Are you ready for this?"

I stare at the ground and shake my head slowly as my mom walks into the room.

"Steven. How are you?" she asks cautiously.

"Okay, Janice. This has knocked me for a real loop, but I'm sleeping better, now that my girl is on the mend."

"Yes, she's tough." Mom caresses my back. "Would you like something to drink?"

"Just some water," Dad says.

I start to giggle, knowing Ray would be happy we're not rolling out the red carpet for even him. Anything to lighten the mood here. Mom looks at me and her laugh kicks in, too—our private joke.

The outburst helps cut the tension my dad brought in with him, on top of our already frayed nerves about this meeting with Brandon and his parents.

We walk into the kitchen. Ray stands to greet my dad. They shake hands and make small talk while I fetch four glasses, filling one with water from the Brita to hand to my dad. Then I pour myself a glass, as well.

Mom grabs two glasses in one hand and the water pitcher in the other. It sloshes against the ice cubes as we head into the living room together. Dad sits next to my mom on the sofa, while I choose the chair across from the coffee table and smile at them as they sink awkwardly into the cushions.

"So," my dad says, smoothing his tan pants with both hands. "This is happening."

We sit silently. In the next room, my brothers talk animatedly about their friend P. J.'s birthday party tomorrow, which promises hours of jumping in a bouncy pirate ship.

The doorbell rings. "I'll get it," Ray's voice booms from the kitchen before his heavy footsteps stride toward the front door. After terse greetings are exchanged, he says, "They are in the living room."

As I stand and swivel, Brandon and his parents enter the room. He is wearing a dark-gray suit over a white button-down shirt and a yellow-and-blue striped tie, and he's carrying a small plastic container. His left eye is still a bit dark and puffy, but other than that, he looks, well, hot as ever.

As the adults stiffly shake hands and then stand silently, I wave a small hello his way. He returns my gesture then sits in the chair across from mine, stashing the box under his seat. His parents arrange themselves on two dining room chairs Ray set up beside the coffee table, opposite my parents.

Once we're all seated, awkwardness fills the air.

"So," my dad says. "This is happening."

* * *

BRANDON

I smile at Alli's dad. His comments break the heaviness apart.

"How are you, Alli?" my mom asks, turning in her direction.

"Yes, Alli, we've been praying for your recovery," my dad says, and I know this is his heartfelt way of saying he cares. I nod in agreement.

Alli perks up. "I'm doing so well, really. My kneecap just got out of alignment. I'm getting physical therapy three times a week. The doctor thinks I'll be ready for training with my team by July."

"Thank goodness," my mom answers. "We have been so upset, so worried. I just want your family to know how sorry we all are."

"Well, this is Brandon's fault, ma'am," Alli's dad barks. "There is nothing you could have done. He was the one driving."

I start to talk but Dad silences me for the moment with a hand zipping his lips.

"Yes, that is true," my mom says. "Brandon definitely is responsible for this horrible, terrible accident. He caused it. But I confused things, I know that." She pauses to pick an invisible piece of lint off her black pants. "I did it because I love my son, but also because I was worried about his questioning. About his possibly turning away from our values. He's my baby, but he's also an adult. He made an adult mistake. And I made one, too. We both have to live with that and learn from it."

"Thank you, Nancy, for your honesty" Alli's mom says. "That must be hard to admit. I know, for me, this has been a real struggle, to watch my daughter wounded. Hurt."

"You've got that right," her dad, Steven, spits out sharply. "They could have been seriously injured. Or worse." Steven pauses, and my blood goes cold as he bores into me with his eyes wild with anger. He nods vigorously and opens his mouth to say more, but Janice pats his knee, prodding him to stop, before he blurts out anything he may regret.

"Steven is taking this all really hard," Alli's mom explains. "I am sure you can understand."

I hesitate, not sure the speech I practiced more than a dozen times in front of my bedroom mirror will keep Alli's dad from wanting to deck me. But I slowly stand up and face her parents, knowing there's no escape. As much as I wish it would, the floor's not going to swallow me whole. I need to go through with what brought us all face to face.

"There is not a minute that has gone by since all this happened that I don't feel like a failure," I say, just as I'd practiced. But quickly, my words stop being an act.

"I failed Alli. I failed you. I failed my parents. And I also failed myself. I understand your anger, your rage. I deserve all of it. But I hope I can also earn your trust again. Alli has been the best part of high school for me. Not just dating her but knowing her. She's incredible."

I turn to face her. "Alli, I need to tell you some things." I lean down and snatch the plastic box from the floor. I open it and fish out a vanilla cookie that I place on a napkin from the box. The cookie is shaped like an S and frosted in blue icing.

She gazes at the sad S and giggles. "That looks like something my brothers would make."

"I baked these cookies. Frosted them, too. Not from scratch, but still. I want to tell you how I feel." One by one, I take out cookie after cookie and gently arrange them on napkins on the table.

Soon the word SORRY is spelled out in crudely-shaped dough shimmering with sky-blue icing.

I face Alli's parents again. "My parents have taken away my driver's license for six months, which I know I deserve. I've learned a lot from this nightmare."

Then I turn toward Alli. "Alli, I know I may have blown my chance to have you in my life. But I don't want your memories of senior year to be all about the accident and what that has meant for you and your family. I would like us to make some better memories than that, starting now, if you'd allow me to be your friend again. And take you to prom. But as friends. Just think about it."

Her dad glares at me as I talk. He's so pissed.

"Mr. Barnett, I know I screwed up so royally. I'm not a bad person. Really, I'm not." I address him directly. "Alli is so important to me. I cannot imagine not having her in my life."

"Dad," Alli says softly, "give it a chance. This is my decision, my choice to hang out with Brandon. Or not."

Oh, damn. That doesn't sound promising. If Alli doesn't want anything to do with me, I will hold my head high and accept that. She has every reason to never want to talk to me again. Still, if there was an ideal time for my prayers to be answered, this would be it.

She turns to me. "Brandon, thank you for all this." She looks at my parents. "I appreciate you both being here today. This is all so difficult. But the good news is, I'm much better." Then she swings her gaze back over to me. "And you're kinda winning me over, Brandon. I have a lot to think about. Prom…" She blows out air as she stops talking and glances at the cookies on the table. The letters that spell *SORRY* neatly aligned. "I don't know if prom works for me. But I want to find a way forward, I do. So, let's try. As friends. Baby steps." She looks at her parents. "Would you be okay if Brandon and I talk things through privately this weekend?"

"You are not to be in a car with him or any of his friends," Alli's dad growls. "Got that?" he directs at Brandon.

"Of course, of course," I answer. "Thank you, sir. Alli, I'll text you later." She nods, and I feel my burden melting slowly away.

"So, does anyone want to try my cookies?" I ask sincerely. "My mom helped me cut them. I messed up a bunch of letters. The O was the hardest, actually. I know it looks more like a blob."

"Yes, I'm afraid my kids take after me. I don't have a Martha Stewart bone in my body," Mom says, rambling.

Alli's mom breaks a piece off the S, pops it into her mouth, and chews. I grab the sorry-looking O and bite into it. My parents each grab an R and take a small nibble. We all stare at the Y sitting there, alone. Alli picks it up and breaks off a corner, handing it to her dad, who holds it at a distance. I lick the icing off the top of my cookie. Alli's mom sets some glasses in a row and fills each with water from the pitcher. We all grab one to wash down the gluey cookies.

The napkins on the coffee table now hold mostly crumbs, other than the broken Y Alli's dad slyly placed back down seconds after his daughter handed it to him.

"Alli's chocolate chip cookies are a lot better, I know," I remark.

"You think?" Alli says smugly. She walks over to her mom and dad and plunks herself down between them on the sofa, her brace clunking softly against the coffee table.

The room is quiet, but the heaviness has dissipated. The distance between our families has maybe not evaporated, but it does seem less insurmountable.

One of Alli's brothers walks into the room and glances around at the six faces. "Tommy, say hi to our guests," his mom says. He smiles at me and then my parents. I give him a small wave. "Hi," he says, staring at me with big brown eyes before he notices what's on the coffee table.

"*Mmm*, cookies." Tommy scrambles closer then pops one of the larger crumbs into his mouth. He frowns at Alli. "These are gross!" Then he gags into his open palm and runs out of the room.

"So," Alli says, looking around the room with a wide grin. "This happened."

*　*　*

ALLI

As Dad is leaving, he stops suddenly and faces me with a serious scowl on his face.

"Dad, you okay? I think this was good, don't you?"

"Ah, sure," he says, pausing. "If you think so, then I do, too." His voice lightens into a positive vibe for the first time tonight. I want to believe this means the anger he displayed during our intense powwow in the living room has slipped away. The dark bags below his eyes reveal how much this has sapped him. He has been so deeply invested in every aspect of my life, and I own up to the fact that my drama has worn him out.

"For dinner tomorrow night, I'd like to bring Padma. Is that all right with you?" he asks, his eyes brightening.

"Yes, that's so great. I'd love to meet her."

"Okay, good. It's settled then." He hugs me tight. "Padma's been a real rock for me. She's helping me find my way through all this. And I'm learning a lot about myself. Did you know I can paint?"

"*Uh*, really?" I'm baffled as to where this is heading.

"Padma signed us up for an evening painting class at the Art Institute with one of her daughter's favorite teachers. I'm not terrible." Dad puffs up his chest a bit, clearly happy to share his achievement with me.

"I can't wait to see your artwork. Will you show me?"

"Yes. Of course. I'm painting mostly objects from the pawnshop that catch my eye. And some scenery. We'll see where it goes. Anyway. This was good tonight. I'm glad we did this. I wasn't sure what to expect. I understand a bit more what you like about Brandon.

He's not a phony. And he's wild about you. Still, I'm not on board yet. This is a time to focus on yourself. What you need. I'm not sure dating someone who's a gun nut is the right choice."

"Dad. He's not a gun nut. We believe different things. But he's not crazy."

"For the record, I don't think Brandon's crazy." His voice is in a higher pitch, as he wags his pointer finger in the air. I know from past experience he's trying to turn this comment into a bad Marx Brothers imitation. My dad's jokes are always a miss. Always! It's one of the things I love about him, how he tries so hard and has no idea how corny he is. "I've raised a kid who's smart and sensible," he adds, back to his serious dad tone, "so I'll leave it at that."

I'm just happy to hear him step back and give me the space to figure out what I want.

"Thanks, Dad. That means so much to hear you say you trust me with this." We hug a second time, and he turns to leave, closing the door softly behind him.

I start to skip into the kitchen, but then, oh yeah. I'm stopped in my tracks by my brace. I stomp in quickly, instead.

"Mom, guess what!" I say loudly.

She's sitting at the table with a small plate of meatballs, a weary expression on her face. "What now, bub? I'm pretty wiped, so no more drama today, please."

"Dad has a girlfriend, her name's Padma, and I'm gonna meet her tomorrow night. His first girlfriend."

"Alli, I hate to break it to you, but Padma is not his first girlfriend. She's the first girlfriend you've met. The first one he's told you about."

"How do you know?"

"Well, for starters, because he dated one of my college friends for two years. It's part of the reason we don't get along so well still. Right after we got divorced, he started going out with Robin. She's always had a thing for lost puppies. So, I told them both that puppy thing, and it didn't go down so well. In my defense, I was pissed."

"Wow, Mom. Your life was like a soap opera."

She laughs. "Not exactly. Though I did spend hours crying by my daughter's hospital bed not too long ago. That's pretty textbook soap opera," she says, adding, "Now come eat some dinner."

I grab a plate and scoop out some meatballs and rotini noodles smothered in tomato sauce. Then I sprinkle it with a liberal dusting of Bragg Nutritional Yeast.

"Yuck," my mom says, crinkling her nose at the yellow powder covering my meal.

I eye the Diet Coke she's drinking with dinner. It's likely her third or fourth of the day. Mom's never embraced any of the health food additions to our kitchen I've picked up from being around Cam all these years: the morning shots of apple cider vinegar, my Vitamin D fixation, and, most of all, the daily protein shakes fortified with spinach, avocado, and turmeric powder.

"*Yum,*" I answer, sliding next to her before I grab a fork and dig in.

* * *

BRANDON

As we walk down the front steps together from Alli's house, I know I have to address what went down just five minutes ago. I'm not going to let my relationship with Alli be defined by my one stupid move— even if that move did leave us with a hurricane of a mess to clean up and fix. I believe what we have is worth fighting for.

"I didn't mean to dump that prom thing on everyone. I'd been thinking about it since I left the hospital. I want this to play out on our terms. I want a second chance with Alli, even if we're just friends. That's fine with me."

"Oh, my dear," Mom says, turning to face me steps from Alli's front door. "You're so young and foolish. There are some battles that are just not worth fighting. I worry you're getting your hopes up about you and her patching things up."

"Mom, not everything is war and peace. Sometimes, there's a gray zone. That's where we are now. I want to get unstuck. I know it will go either way. But I'm willing to chance it."

"Nancy, let the boy be. He's made up his mind."

"Well, we do have a big surprise for you," Mom adds as we settle into the car. "Something to lighten the mood. Ready?"

She turns around in the front passenger seat to face me, her arm on my knee. "Maura is coming home for your graduation. The school granted her request for a ten-day vacation. She's flying fourteen hours to be here, so we can celebrate as a family."

I smile huge. A weeklong dose of Maura is the best medicine for my parents right now. The house needs some of her energy in it. She's the storyteller in the family. And living in Japan has supplied her with an endless number of laughs and amazements. Like how the kids in Japan have a comic superhero named the Butt Detective, who solves crimes and *really* looks like a butt!

"Maura says she's buying me a genuine Japanese karaoke machine for graduation, whether I want one or not. She's obsessed," I share with my parents, so happy to have changed the subject to a new topic for the car ride home.

* * *

ALLI

Brandon texts me on Sunday afternoon.

> *My wheels these days are the skateboard kind. That only gets me so far. Are you driving yet? I was hoping you come over one day this week.*

I sit with his text. I want to respond, *YES*. I want to respond now. But I need to be cautious. *Don't I?*

I decide to turn on the TV and watch an episode I taped of one of my new favorite shows, *90 Day Fiancé*, and whip through my twenty physical therapy exercises. Okay, maybe it's ten, but it is a lot. After that, I'll respond. I'll say *YES*!

I watch two people who should never get married figure that out at the eleventh hour. *Phew!* Divorce and misery averted.

I finish most of my prescribed exercises. And then I text Brandon. But not a *YES*.

Driving fine. I just need to keep my left leg mostly straight.

I take a break to text my mom a question and wait for her response before sending over a new message.

Mom says I can use her car on Tuesday. She's home early.

That's me being subtle. I've had a week of uncertainty and doctor visits since getting out of the hospital. Although I've had time to stew and an opportunity grow into my hate for Brandon, my mind never went to that dark place. Instead, I realized one big truth after he left the other night, leaving his napkin of cookie crumbs behind. I want prom to be with him. When I imagine myself there, it's with Brandon by my side. There is nobody else who could be in that picture.

My phone pings.

We're going to Mario's. See you at 6.

Dad texts like I don't have this imprinted in my brain. It's *always* Sunday. *Always* at 6.

Next up is meeting the girlfriend. Dinner with Dad and Padma. I'm excited to be a witness to what I imagine and hope is their wonderful, heart-stopping love. With any luck, my dad will be in the throes of it, so he will respect my desire for forgiveness and will accept that even a car accident, staring down two months of rehab, and almost losing my opportunity to swim at Miami-Ohio hasn't doomed me and Brandon.

He's made it clear he's uncomfortable with Brandon's attitude about gun ownership. But he needs to understand I won't let that overshadow what Brandon and I have together. We have a lot to learn from each other. To teach each other. I realize he's been steeped in his family's values that have shaped him into the person he is today. A person with a strong moral code, who values family and honors his word. And I like that person. A ton!

My phone pings again. Brandon has thumbed up my text.

* * *

BRANDON

At 4 p.m., I sit down in the wingback chair in our living room nearest the front door and wait for the doorbell to ring. Astor scampers up next to me, yearning to be petted, so I oblige. It's just me and the dog and a loudly ticking clock on the living room mantel in an otherwise quiet house. And soon, Alli will make three.

I hear her walking up the front steps and bound out of my chair as she knocks softly on the front door.

Opening it, I grin foolishly at her. She's wearing jeans and a long-sleeve black Dri-FIT shirt. As she walks in, she pauses inches from my face.

"Hi," she says faintly. Astor runs over and rubs her nose against the brace. Alli bends down and scratches the top of her head.

I move in to hug her. "How are you?"

"I swam yesterday. For physical therapy. It was great."

"That's awesome."

We walk over to the family room sofa and plunk down at the same time, side by side. The dog jumps up next to me.

"Scoot, Astor," I say, pushing her down from the couch cushions. As she scampers away, I turn to look at Alli, and our lips connect quickly, passionately. I lean closer, so my chest presses against hers. She lies back to welcome it.

Soon, we're 100-percent horizontal. We take it slow, because we can, and because her fragile left leg demands it. What comes next is heat and light. Pure fireworks.

* * *

ALLI

"Maybe we should have talked before we did that," I say, laughing, as I come back from the bathroom fully dressed and sit back down next to him on the sofa.

"So, let's talk now," I continue, before I lose my nerve. "Parkland and March for our Lives have changed something in me from who I was when we first got together. I know you have a history and comfort with guns that I will never understand. But I don't want to blow up our whole relationship because of one topic where we aren't on the same page. I don't want to be surrounded only by people who are carbon copies of myself."

Brandon nods eagerly. "Agreed." He kisses me again smack on the lips. "What comes now?"

"April 20, I want us both to talk at the march outside the high school. I'm going to speak from the heart. I'm going to be honest. And I want you to, also."

"Yeah, I've seen the flyers about that. My mom will kill me," he says quickly.

"Brandon. You're eighteen. Don't do it if you don't want to. But don't make your mom the excuse, either," she adds, fingering the small silver dolphin I gave her for Valentine's Day.

"It's complicated with my mom. In Desert Storm, she experienced things I will never understand. She still has a hard time coping with stressful situations. And this is all very stressful for her."

I stare at him, letting his words sink in. "Oh. I'm sorry. I wish you had told me that earlier. Let's forget it then."

"Although *maybe* I can say something at the march, something I believe in and my classmates would understand, too. Be that other voice, like you said. Let me see what I can come up with. I'll ask Jimmy to help me. He did rock it on debate team freshman year."

"Perfect. I'll clear it with Justine and make sure she's game. She'll need to give her thumbs-up to what you want to say."

"I figured that. Justine does like me, though. I helped her survive junior year Algebra Trig, and she helped me get through Advanced Spanish."

"I wouldn't count on any special treatment from Justine. She's on a mission. You have a tough assignment, but I'll fight for you. We need to hear from different voices. You've taught me that. Just don't piss anyone off."

Brandon laughs. "Well, she's not the only one on a mission. My mom is, too, it seems. I've become her mission."

"Oh really?" I sit quietly with this information. "So, what does that mean? Am I the enemy in this scenario?"

"You could never be the enemy. You're my Alli," Brandon says, rushing the words. "Even my mom gets that." I melt a little at the tenderness in his voice.

I lean into him on the sofa and extend my good leg over his lap. "How is your mom doing?" I ask, gently. "This has been hard for both our families."

"Her focus is not on you, I promise. It's me," he says, stroking my thigh softly. "I've stepped up more at home. I've even stopped bitching about mowing the lawn. And she's so excited about me going to Wisconsin that we've been talking a lot about the future. That helps."

Astor rushes back into the room with a bone in her mouth and drops it at my feet. I pick it up and throw it a few feet away, for her to fetch, then wipe the wet drool residue on my jeans. As I start to push myself upright, my braced leg puts me a bit off balance, and Brandon jumps to his feet to help me stand up.

"Yeah. My parents are being really hyper about my recovery, so I get it," I say. "I better go. My mom needs the car to pick my brothers up from karate."

"Sure. Well. Thanks for making this work. I'm glad we're an us again."

"Me, too. And I can't wait to read your speech."

"Okay... I'll show you mine, if you show me yours."

"Deal," I say.

Brandon walks me to the door, and I feel his eyes follow me as I step slowly and carefully back to the minivan.

* * *

BRANDON

Alli and I spend the next week going back and forth on Google Docs, making suggestions and changes, until we're both satisfied with what we each have to say at the rally. I fully admit I hadn't thought it through, when I jumped at going down this road with her. I eagerly grabbed at the chance to ease my guilt over the pain I'd caused. I didn't want to lose what we'd just gotten back. What at first felt like a mistake quickly morphed into putting myself front and center in this strange new world of speaking out.

Two surprising things followed: I didn't hate it. Even better? Alli and I are tighter than ever.

I prepare for one of the hardest things I've ever done in my life, coming a close second to the drama I rained down on us all after the car accident. I need to share this speech with my parents. I recognize the box I've built for myself, with tonight's surprise announcement arriving only weeks after the mess the three of us have been busy cleaning up.

I make sure to catch them at a good time: while they're eating bowls of ice cream in front of their newest TV binge. Last month, my mom's sister, Liza, came for a long weekend visit and told them straight out she didn't want to discuss or watch anything political. They settled on a few quiet nights in front of *Mad Men*, and my parents now have an expanded TV universe, which we all welcome. They are only on the second season of a show with another seventy-plus episodes to go.

I settle myself strategically next to my dad on the sofa. "Do you know what April 20 is?" I ask them, knowing full well they have no idea where I'm coming from. "It's the anniversary of the Columbine shooting and also National School Walkout Day. There's a rally at school Friday. I wrote a speech that I hope I'm going to give, and I wanted you to read it first."

"Is this something Alli suggested?" my mom asks, peering knowingly at me over her wire-rimmed glasses. She picks up the remote and pauses the action on the screen.

I nod repeatedly, ready to defend my role. "Don't you think it's important for different voices to have their say? That's all I'm trying to do. To feel included in this, not excluded."

"That actually sounds reasonable," my dad says, sliding his bowl of ice cream over to the coffee table and extending his arm toward me. "Let's see where this goes then."

I hand over the words I've polished to a shine. My parents read them together slowly, my dad holding the page as my mom peers over his shoulder.

When they are both done, Dad swiftly hands the paper back to me.

"Most of what you've written, I just don't agree with," Mom says in protest, as I expected. "You do realize this contradicts the Libertarian platform in so many ways."

"Exactly," my dad complains. "Why don't you take another look at the paragraph where you say the age to own guns should be higher. That it's up to your generation to make that happen. I'm just a bit surprised at how strongly you criticize our current government and also how you endorse more regulation."

I sit still, waiting for more grumbling, expecting nothing less from them than honesty.

Then *both* my parents proceed to say the coolest words that have ever come out of their mouths.

"A few years ago, I worked with a veteran, Martin, who wanted to go to law school," my mom begins. "He was searching for a paralegal job, because he didn't know how he could become a lawyer with two kids and a wife and a mortgage. I helped him find a good position not far from where he lived. Last week, he called me out of the blue to tell me he's going to law school in the fall. That he has to follow his heart, not his head. That's what he said. His wife got a promotion, and his family's going to tighten their belts for three years and make it work. It wouldn't be right if I didn't tell you the same thing I told him. That you have to live your life authentically, and the rest will follow. We love and support you, so, if this is what you need to do, then do it."

"So, let me get this right," I joke with her. "You told Martin that you love and support him?"

"No. Of course not," she says, her eyes smiling. "Look. It's been an eventful month, and you being in the hospital really put a lot of priorities in perspective. Now I'm going to borrow a phrase from your sister, Kelly. See what I learn from these kids?" She glances at my dad for a brief second before announcing proudly, "Brandon, you do you."

Dad rests his hand on my mom's knee and chimes in. "That's good advice, son. You know what Ayn Rand would say about all this?" When he looks from me to Mom, we both shake our heads.

He sits straighter on the sofa and delivers one of his Ayn Rand-isms. "The question isn't who is going to let me; it's who is going to stop me." Then he leans back into the sofa, pleased he was able to inject classic Libertarian philosophy into our discussion.

"Okay, Mom, Dad. So, this is for real?" I hesitate when they stare at me blankly. "You're not mad?"

"You'll be in college in a few months," Dad says. "We've taught you our value system. Now, it's up to you how you want to live that."

Mom picks up the remote and looks up to see if I have anything to add, before she presses play. "Dear, our ice cream is melting. We're fine, I promise," she says, eyeing the mushy mint-green blob in the bowl on her lap.

She seems on the verge of being annoyed about my continuing to interrupt their evening's plans. Then she settles back into the sofa cushion and sighs. "I get that your generation sees things differently. I can't fault you for that."

"Thanks. This is great," I announce and briefly hug them both before bolting up to call Alli.

I press her name on my Favorites bar. She's expecting an update tonight and picks up on the first ring.

"My parents are strangely okay with my speech," I tell her. "They went all hippie about being authentic to myself. It was weird."

"My parents were strange about all this, too," she says. "I told my dad, and he basically asked me to keep him updated, like maybe it won't all happen. And then my mom made it sound like I'd snagged the lead in a play. She just didn't get it. She said my middle school acting days were good preparation for this role. I didn't bother explaining to her I'm not playing a role. It's not worth it."

"You got it worse than I did!" I exclaim. "Hey, what shows were you in? I was one of the Lost Boys in *Peter Pan* in seventh grade. For a minute, I thought acting could be my thing, but I wasn't too good."

"Me, either," she says. "I was in a play in seventh grade, too. I was one of the mean stepsisters in *Cinderella*. And also, my cousin and I were in *Seussical* together one summer at sleep-away camp. I played

Mrs. Mayor. But I can't sing or dance, so I figured I should stick to swimming."

"You know, your dad actually makes a good point," I say. "We shouldn't get ahead of ourselves, because we still have to get the okay from our supreme leader."

"That's true. Justine can be a real P-I-T-A when she wants to be," Alli states. "Well, if we do pull this together, I'm afraid my mom's going to be there to hear us. She even freaked me out and said she was going to wear the pink pussy hat her sister Kay gave her as a present, when she was trying to convince Mom to attend the Women's March in Chicago with her, which my mom didn't end up doing. I think she's been waiting for an event where she could put it to use. I was about to be pissed at her cluelessness, but then she fessed up that she wouldn't do that to me, that she was joking. Funny, huh?" She giggles.

I conjure up the ridiculous image of Alli's mom wearing her pink hat with the cat ears, standing in the midst of our classmates, and I smile into my cellphone.

"The question I keep asking myself is, do I even belong up there on Friday?" I confess. "You read what I've written. It's not the liberal lingo everyone is expecting."

"Brandon, your speech is not that far out. Really. You aren't the anarchist you think you are."

"Says you. Let's see if Justine agrees."

* * *

ALLI

Brandon and I sit our butts down across from Justine at a long table in the school library, minutes after the final bell, both of us holding our heartfelt words stamped on paper. We've jumped through some pretty big hoops so far. There's only one left.

She reads Brandon's one-page, single-spaced offering and then eagerly picks up my two pages full of exclamation points and words in ALL CAPS.

After slowly reading through the sentences Brandon and I sweated over, separately and together, Justine splits my two pages and slides Brandon's one slim sheet in between them. Then she folds the papers in half and sets them on the table. Our eyes follow every one of her deliberate movements. She pushes them over to where we sit side by side.

"Do this," she says and then clams shut.

"Do *what*?" I finally ask. I'm super-confused.

"Say this together. Not separately. Not one by one. This needs to be one speech. One beautiful epic speech that you deliver together," she explains.

"So, let me get this right. You want our message mashed together?" Brandon asks.

"Yes. Can you make that work?" she says, and I hear a challenge in her tone.

Justine must know that challenging an athlete to anything will yield only one answer.

Without missing a beat, Brandon gazes at me and nods with his chin just once before he gently fist-bumps me under the table.

"Sure, Justine. We've got this," I respond.

* * *

APRIL 20

BRANDON

Here we are. Shoulder to shoulder on our school's front steps. How is it that Alli and I are the ones standing up for sanity and our generation in this moment? How is it I'm *that* person? The one whom my peers are looking to for answers.

I study the scene before me. Many, many people gaze expectantly our way. A sea of ripped jeans, sweatshirts, and homemade signs, all waiting to be inspired by what we have to say.

Justine and Graham, a junior I've passed in the hallways a hundred times but never spoken to, stand in front of us, leading a chant.

Graham shouts into the microphone, "WHAT DO WE WANT?"

The whole, jacked-up crowd responds in unison, "CHANGE!"

"WHEN DO WE WANT IT?" Justine bellows, raucously.

"NOW!" erupts hundreds of voices.

The shoutouts continue back and forth, while two other students, Imani and Kelvin, stand beside Graham and Justine like bookends, each holding up huge, white poster boards that display photos and names of the seventeen students and teachers who were killed on February 14 at Marjory Stoneman Douglas High School, surrounded by dozens of pink, scribbled hearts.

A quiet begins to settle over the crowd.

"WE ARE THE CHANGE!" announces a fired-up Justine. The five of us stand alongside her, each of us in a dark-gray T-shirt with

#ENOUGH splayed across the front in white letters, compliments of Ms. Arnold.

"Now we want to introduce you to our final speakers, seniors Alli and Brandon," Graham yells into the microphone above the fading din.

As we step forward, we hear whispers, random rustlings, and some hollers.

"We all want the same thing," Alli begins. The microphone carries her voice forward and out over the mass of students. "Hey, Brandon, what's that thing we want again?" She turns slightly in my direction.

"Oh, yeah. I got this." With both my arms outstretched, I say, "You mean to feel safe in our school?" Then I take a deep breath, fold my arms, and follow the script. "You know, I support the Second Amendment." As I stand there, I receive the huge chorus of boos I'd been expecting.

I yell over the disapproval. "But that doesn't mean I don't want to feel safer! I think politicians need to be more reasonable. An eighteen-year-old should *not* have an assault rifle."

"Exactly," Alli says after me, just as we rehearsed a dozen times. The stirred-up crowd quiets down. "It's time to stop talking about sensible gun legislation but never *do* anything about it." Then she shrugs her shoulders and asks me, "So, how do we get there?"

"I want to protect the right to go hunting with my dad, but why would a teenager need to buy a handgun or a semi-automatic weapon?" I ask, scanning the crowd for a response. Students cheer and shout—though I do hear a few boos mixed in from my throwing out the word "hunting." "Our country needs mental health reform!" I continue loudly, to the roar of more support.

"Hey!" Alli taps me theatrically on the shoulder. "I have one. Universal background checks!" Then she adds, "Or what about closing the loopholes in private gun sales? Or—I'm going to be really crazy here, go really wild—what about an assault weapon ban?"

I shake my head back and forth. That was the one line we couldn't agree on. The word *ban* just stings a Second Amendment supporter to the core. But she insisted, and since the sentiment isn't coming from me, what can I do?

The crowd jumps up and down, screaming like we're rock stars.

"My turn," I announce. "Register to vote and then *vote*! Because, right now, politicians are failing to keep us safe."

"We could even go further," Alli adds, full-out dramatic. "Hey, get this. We could contact our representative!"

"Good point! Smart thinking!" I tap the side of my head. Then we both look out at the crowd and nod our heads in unison.

"So, you mean we can make our voices heard then?" Alli asks me, speaking directly into the microphone.

"Yes, I believe we can." I peek at one of my index cards, to make sure I am on target with what comes next.

"How about we work with our elected leaders to approve sensible gun laws?" she says, her voice rising and her right arm pointing into the crowd.

I pivot toward her, "But what if what is sensible to you isn't sensible to me?" My words spill out just as we practiced, and I drop the index card. I've got this.

"We have to begin somewhere. I don't want to trample on your rights, but don't you trample on mine," Alli proclaims. "And I'm just getting started."

"Okay. *Geez...* Go ahead, then." I stick my hands up and back away, giving her the floor.

She steps grandly in front of me. "This time is different than before. Don't you think?" she asks the mass of animated faces in front of us.

People yell and hold their signs higher. They say, FEAR HAS NO PLACE IN SCHOOL and #NOT ONE MORE.

"What makes it different, though, Alli? What's different about *now*?" I ask, leaning into the microphone to make sure I'm heard.

"You *know* the answer. We've been talking about it for two months. We students have *power*."

I step back in line alongside her, so together we stand front and center.

Alli shouts into the microphone as she waves her hands outward, "NOT JUST THOUGHTS. NOT JUST PRAYERS. CHANGE!"

As she starts to back away, I make my fingers into a V and launch my hand high. This wasn't in the script, so Alli makes a sudden turn to watch me yell, "*Peace out!*"

Whooping and hollering follow our final words. Justine rushes toward us and raises both her hands above her head for high-fives all around. *"That's what I'm talking about!"* she exclaims, beaming.

We slip behind Justine and Graham, so they can close out the rally.

"We done good!" I yell to Alli, hoping she can hear me over the commotion.

"Real good!" she answers. After we drop down from the steps, she says, "Guess what?"

I stop in my tracks. "What, Alli?"

For a hot second, she playfully presses two fingers into my chest in the same V shape I just displayed to half my classmates.

"You're so not a nerd." She flashes me her moonshot smile.

"I hope it didn't take you this long to figure that out." I sweep her into my grasp and land a kiss.

How did I get here?

I'm amazed at what I just said, did, and accomplished. I don't recognize myself right now. When we were rehearsing, it was all make-believe. But now, I've bared my soul in front of my school and survived it.

I also learned something of substance, now that I've successfully stepped into the fray. I can be pro-gun *and* engaged in this movement, to change what I see is broken. I have a voice and a vote, and I intend to use them both, so kids no longer have to worry about getting shot in their classroom.

* * *

ALLI

We navigate the crush of bodies coming at us from every which way, as students begin to scatter and head back to class. My left knee is throbbing but only slightly, which is good news. I chose to keep my brace off this morning, but now I'm suffering the consequences.

Tyler walks up to us, his contorted face inches from Brandon.

"What the fuck was that?" he says. "I thought you were cooler than that. Now you're up there spouting all that left-wing bullshit."

"I'm not into labels. Don't put those on me, man," Brandon says, his face reddening slightly as he pulls away from Tyler's storm of words. I stand back, not wanting to be in the middle of their disagreement.

"I just expected something better from you. Your girl has made you soft," Tyler says then turns and walks away. Conversation over.

"Whoa! That was ridiculous," I say.

"He doesn't know shit," Brandon says.

"I guess Tyler was expecting you to go all out Rambo today."

Brandon shrugs and looks down. "Hey, you didn't wear your brace. I just noticed."

"Yeah, I probably needed to. But I don't feel too bad, actually."

A hand touches my right shoulder and I spin around. My mom and dad are standing smack in front of me.

"This is a surprise," I say. Truer words have not been spoken.

My dad hugs me tight while my mom steps back and lets him have this moment. "You did amazing," he says.

"Dad! I didn't expect you here. And with mom, too." I try to digest this alien invasion of my parents hanging together in the middle of the day at my school walkout.

"Janice invited me," Dad says. "And how could I miss this? I closed the store for a few hours, and I'm so glad I did. I taped it, too, so you can have it. Brandon, I think your parents would be proud. I'll be happy to send you the video to share."

"I think I'm okay for now," Brandon says. "But thanks. Hello, Mrs. Nixen." He flashes a goofy grin in my mom's direction, as though making sure to gain some brownie points with both my parents. Then he gestures randomly and says, "Hey, Alli, I'm heading over here," making his escape from our family circle. That's fine with me.

"Sure. See you later," I shout after him then ask Mom, "So? How'd I do?"

"I know you may not see it, but you were dynamic and projected really well. I think, the way you presented yourself, people heard you. I certainly did."

"What did you hear?"

"Well, to be honest, I only vote in presidential elections," she admits. "I'm going to fix that."

"What about you, Dad?"

"You were both great. Really powerful. I'm impressed by Brandon. Maybe he's not the boy I thought he was. I'm still upset about you getting hurt, of course, but I see he's trying to figure a lot out. I guess we all are, aren't we?"

"Damn straight we are," my mom replies.

We all laugh, three voices rising together in a joyful pitch, and it's music to my ears. Anyone looking over at us would think we're just a normal, happy family.

* * *

EPILOGUE

MAY 19

BRANDON

Jimmy and I have dominated in a friendly game of Ultimate once again.

"I'm gonna miss us slaying," he says as we collapse on the grass, exhilarated by having our senior regulars trounce the juniors, who have now gathered in a tight pack nearby, most of them ignoring us by checking their Instagram feeds or drinking from water bottles.

"Man, the band has to split up one day, right?" I announce to Marco, Brett, and Kyle.

"No. You could have come to U of I with me," Jimmy answers.

"I can say the same about Wisconsin."

"Shut up, you two," says Marco, pushing himself up to standing. "You're being drama queens. We've got prom in a few hours, so I'm gonna go clean up." His grass-stained knees are a sorry sight.

Brett, sitting inches away, says point-blank, "I still can't believe Alli took you back. That's just crazy of her."

I look straight at him. "You're probably right. But I'm not living in the past. I'm focused on now."

"Confucius say," jokes Brett as he bobs his head around. "I'm rooting for you two. Really! I'm just kinda shocked how that accident majorly messed up her knee, and now you're going to prom together."

"Now who's the drama queen?" Marco interjects, raking his fingers through his shaggy black hair. "Leave the guy alone. He's already suffered a ton."

I let it go, and I'm glad Brett does, too. He's not my favorite guy, which is a nice way of saying I think he can be a jackass, but he's super-fast, so Jimmy put him on our Ultimate group chat sophomore year.

"See you at five at my house," Jimmy says, extending a hand to help me up off the ground. He's been driving me everywhere these days, while I've forked over a lot of gas money to make sure he keeps doing it. "My mom bought a huge box of pigs-in-a-blanket from Costco. If you want to be a little hungry or something, that's good."

"Wieners at Jimmy's at five. See you, man," says Kyle as he jumps up from the grass and grabs his string bag. "I'll be there."

* * *

ALLI

PROM NIGHT, 5:30 P.M.

There's no way my mom was going to let me get into a car with Brandon and his friends before prom. Therefore, I'm sitting in the back seat of the Audi behind my stepdad, who is driving, while my mom nervously chatters from the passenger seat. I can tell she's not ready to let me have this much freedom again, even though Brandon and I have done everything possible to make our parents comfortable with our prom weekend plans.

The guys have preordered two UberXLs to arrive at Jimmy's at 6:30 p.m. and drive the twelve of us to our prom at the Marriott in Chicago. And, thankfully, the lake house is still happening, too! Matt's cousin, Lucy, is going to meet us all outside the hotel at 10 p.m. with the fifteen-person van she rented and drive us up there.

"So, no swimming after dark. Promise me," Mom says. We have discussed every potential pitfall that could befall a person who spends two days and nights with eleven other post-prom high school seniors at a house by the beach in Wisconsin. I am shocked she has come up with any new precautions. I thought we'd covered every possibility. But here it is. She has found another.

"I know," I say, nodding my head yet again to show I do understand her concerns.

Her being a bundle of nerves has not helped calm mine. Brandon and I have already talked honestly and probably too much about the fact that our families hanging at this pre-prom party together is not anyone's idea of a good time. I feel like I deserve, for tonight at least, to be worry-free. But then, real life has a way of butting in to mess with the best-laid plans.

On the plus side, I am so thankful my mom hired a neighborhood teen to watch my brothers for an hour, so we can have this family experience be just about me.

Nervously, I play with my ornate new gold bracelet, sliding the, thick bangle lightly up and down my wrist. Padma insisted I have it, Dad explained. After all, it's the bracelet that brought them together.

"My little girl's all grown up and so very beautiful," he announced as he presented it to me, tucked in a soft, black-velvet pouch, his eyes wet with tears, during last Sunday's 6 p.m. dinner.

"Jimmy told me Brandon was relieved that my doctor's orders are for no dancing," I tell Ray and my mom, hoping to pivot our conversation away from any more danger talks. "He says Brandon moves like the Tinman."

"Sounds like he dances like I do," Ray says, looking at Mom and playfully squeezing her left knee. She laughs before he returns his hand to the steering wheel and he pulls in behind another parked car in front of Jimmy's house.

As I step out, I pick up the white rose boutonniere encased in a small, plastic box. Brandon is standing stiffly in the driveway, looking handsome in his dark suit and deep-blue tie. He strolls over with his own transparent container that holds a white corsage straining against the edges, just waiting to be released.

* * *

BRANDON

PROM NIGHT, 5:30 P.M.

"I'm on my third of these," says Kyle as he violently shakes the upside-down yellow mustard tube before squeezing a big blob on his pig-in-a-blanket. Then he pops the mini-hot dog into his mouth and chews before grabbing a napkin from the buffet table to wipe his lips.

I notice a small, yellow spot on the lapel of his black suit but decide not to say anything about it. He did clean up nice since our Ultimate match a few hours ago, though. I give him props for choosing a skinny, black tie. But I'm not his keeper.

"I can't eat," I admit. "Alli's family is going to be here any minute. I'm sure they still hate me."

"Not today they don't," Kyle says. "Maybe tomorrow, but today they don't want to ruin Alli's night. You should be good."

"So, you think they hate me?"

He nods vigorously.

"Great. You're helping me *not at all.*" I walk away to find a friendlier, more sympathetic face. As I think more about what Kyle said, though, he's probably right on. Still, I'm really glad I didn't tell him he's got a blob of mustard on his suit. Karma is a bitch.

I want to confide in Jimmy. I'm so fricking nervous, and I know I can count on him to tell me some stupid story that will distract me from my own thoughts. I find him smack in the middle of a conversation with his parents and Shelby, whose clingy, floor-length red dress has a slit up one side that doesn't stop until it reaches mid-thigh.

Jimmy's "costume" mirrors mine: black suit with a red tie that matches Shelby's bold fashion choice. Except for our shoes. I've got the requisite black loafers on. He's wearing his dope sneakers: Adidas Icon Nations Baseball Turf high-tops that he told me he spent thirty minutes cleaning with a toothbrush, to make sure they looked brand-spanking new, even though they're not. I know for a fact they were the number-one item on a Christmas list he presented to his parents last December.

I fidget with my phone again, unlocking it to check my Snap Map. From the names under the map icon, I click on Alli's and can see her avatar on a nearby street. Just a tiny sliver away from my location's blob on the map. I start to walk down the driveway toward the front of the house, so I can see her car drive up.

I walk past the huge van in Jimmy's driveway. Inside it, I've stashed a bag with my toothbrush, toothpaste, and deodorant, plus a few T-shirts, shorts, and a bathing suit. Parents have already loaded the back luggage compartment with two coolers filled with burgers, lunch meat, eggs, and milk. Piled on top are massive bags of potato chips, cookies, hamburger buns, and paper Trader Joe's bags filled with more good snacks.

Meeting Alli at Jimmy's was not part of my original plan. But there was no way any of my friends or I would have been allowed to pick her up, and there was no way I was going to drive over here with her parents, the two of us sitting together in the back seat like we were in a fricking sixth-grade carpool.

Anyway, the thing I've learned so much about these past few months is *compromise*. You can't always get what you want. But if you try sometimes, you can get what you need. That may originally be from the Rolling Stones, but it also is the biggest thing I've taken away from my senior year.

I spy the silver Audi pull up to the curb and walk over to it as Alli steps out of the car looking like an angel come down from heaven in her long, blue dress, her normally straight hair falling in loose dark curls around her shoulders.

Suddenly, all is good with the world again. My heartbeat immediately starts to slow down as my nerves evaporate into the warm spring air. Amazingly, my stomach stops doing flips and flops.

Seeing Alli, I know exactly what I need to do.

* * *

ALLI

For me, the craziest, most unexpected truth of this evening is not that Brandon and I are going to prom together.

It's that, so far, I'm actually having a wonderful time, sipping on iced tea and snacking from a vegetable platter as I hang with my friends and our families.

It's that Simone is wearing the bubble-gum-pink dress with the train and rhinestone spaghetti straps and that Daryl caved so now sports a pink bowtie to match.

It's that the dress looks really awesome on her, and I don't even need to wear the sunglasses I brought as a joke.

It's that she owns her radiance, and I'm proud to stand by her side in my sapphire dress from Bloomingdale's, even if she so outshines me.

It's that I'm wearing a bracelet given to me by my dad, who is crazy about the beautiful, caring, and wonderful Padma Alahari.

It's that, in this sun-drenched early evening in Jimmy's backyard, with our parents taking photos nonstop, I watch my mom and Brandon's mom sharing their cell numbers, so they can exchange pictures.

It's that my dad and Ray are standing two feet from each other with smiles on their faces.

It's that today marks day four of me not wearing a brace.

And it's that, when Brandon was slipping the white rose and baby's breath corsage gently on my bare wrist, he leaned in close and whispered in my ear, "I love you, Alli."

When he said it, I wanted to say it right back. But I didn't. That will have to wait. We have all night.

* * *

AUTHOR'S NOTE

Thank you to everyone who helped me in my research, most notably the EMPOWER Club at York Community, and to my early readers. Thank you with all my heart to my family. David, Benjamin and Julia, I treasured having you by my side during this journey as you helped me get the important details just right. Thank you to StoryStudio/NIAY, James Klise, Deborah Halverson, and David Aretha for your writing guidance. Thank you, Kathryn Galán, for putting the finishing touches on this novel. Lastly, thank you to all those now reading these words, as that means you finished reading my novel.

ೞೞೞ

"When you talk, you are only repeating what you already know. But if you listen, you may learn something new.

—The Dalai Lama